Lost Minds, Wandering Souls

Volume 8

By

George Adamczyk

Table of Contents

Ghosts in the Glass

"Be our guest," the song repeated.

Cassie used to treasure the "Beauty and the Beast" movie. It was one of those chosen few that her mother had kept on DVD from her own toddler days. She watched it over and over and over again until her mom finally screamed in frustration and yanked the plug from the TV. Countless others had fallen to the wayside, forgotten classics she once loved, yet now barely remembered. But she always had a soft spot for this old tale of the beautiful girl forced to live with that horrifying beast, even as an eighth grader now more into hip hop and boys at school.

Watching it now, instead of marching around the living room and singing along happily at the top of her voice, she whimpered, tears curling down her velvety cheeks. Burrowed into the corner of her pantry upon that stiff, twin-sized torture device she reluctantly had to use as a mattress. Once upon a time, this was her favorite fairy tale. Now it was a terrifying reminder of how her life had changed for the worse. Cassie had been forced to live with a creature even more frightening than any beast she had ever imagined.

Her own father.

Her Mom had been a ball of perpetual motion, as pretty as she was energetic. Modern enough to understand the latest updates on

Cassie's computer and dance with her to the latest rap hits, yet still old-fashioned enough to wear an apron when she cooked dinner and darn holes in socks instead of tossing them in the trash. Rarely spoke of her own upbringing. Winced when family members brought up old tales of those days. From bits and pieces of stories Cassie had overheard, it seemed her mother married young to get away from a violent home life, only to find herself trapped by a husband who treated her even worse than her daddy. Maybe that's why she was such a whirlwind. Always subconsciously moving to avoid being a sitting target.

And that might also be the reason she died so suddenly. By the time Cassie returned from an after-school dance class that mundane Tuesday, her mom already had homemade stew on the stove and fresh blueberry pie baking in the oven. Those intoxicating smells were now forever burned into Cassie's consciousness. Mom was zooming her sleek blue vacuum cleaner around like a Ferrari on an obstacle course, darting in and out of the tightest spots between the living room furniture without ever banging into the baseboards. A slight smile curled her lips whenever she heard the crackling of large dust particles being sucked in.

Staying as busy as possible kept her home clean and her mind clear. She worked until every ounce of energy her body had been allotted for that day was drained like the coffeemaker, down to the last drop. That way, she would fall asleep the second her cheek hit the pillow, preventing evil memories from haunting her restlessness, transforming into waking nightmares too painful to withstand.

The most frightening thing about life is how its most important moments come without any warning. This seemed like just another routine segment in a never-ending stream of time, of a happiness which felt destined to last forever. No siren blared, no red light flashed to alert her that her very existence was about to be thrust into a bottomless pit of despair.

Cassie never even got to say "Hello." The noise of the motor prevented any final communications between the two. Mom was there one moment and gone the next. Her blithe spirit shone in her eyes as Cassie walked in, but simply vanished a second later. Her soul dissipated before her body hit the floor. The strongest person Cassie ever met, a lady who never got sick and was always there for her, dropped like a safe right next to the rose-colored ottoman. Fell to the carpet as if her batteries had simply worn out. The Energizer Bunny was no more.

Her shocking demise pulled the rug out from under Cassie's entire life. As she watched Mom's lifeless form topple over, her own young life flashed before her eyes. At the very instant all her mother's thoughts deactivated in her brain for the final time, a thousand of Cassie's reflections flickered throughout her own. Cassie knew her beloved lifestyle had perished along with her. No more quiet talks before bedtime. No more hugs of sympathy after a bad day at school. No more words of encouragement when she studied for a test. No more late-night pizza and movies on Saturdays.

Now she had to go live with closest relative, her brutal, neglectful father. A lazy scumbag who basked upon his worn-out recliner as if it were a throne. Always had a joke and a smile for friends and relatives. Nothing but the back of his hand for his wife and kid. House devil, street angel. Avoided work like Clark Kent avoided kryptonite.

Cassie had once asked her mom how on earth she chose him from all the guys in the neighborhood. Mom quivered as if someone had stabbed her voodoo doll in the heart with a pin, then just turned away, mumbling that men change after they get married. But her dad didn't just change, he pulled a complete Jekyll and Hyde. Went from the sweet, attentive guy she'd seen on old videos to beating her and forcing her to have sex. Sometimes right in front of Cassie.

Think of what kind of trauma that would cause to an impressionable five-year-old girl. They say a daughter gets her feelings about men from the way their fathers treated their mothers. Poor Cassie was a car wreck before she could even drive.

Social services came and dragged her away from her mom's apartment. It always smelled so nice, like a lady's home. Cassie had grown accustomed to being greeted by a warm, loving parent whenever she came back from school. She slept in her own queen-sized bed, with a laptop and video games and a small TV on the bureau. The living room was a museum of pretty things. Frilly lace laid under tempered glass on all the tables and shelves. Dolls from all around the world. African, Asian, Hispanic, Native American. All dressed in native clothing, like they were all going to a party at the United Nations.

And her favorite thing of all; a portrait-sized mirror framed in lustrous dark hazelwood. It had been hanging in Cassie's bedroom for as long as she could remember. Mom told her it was for her own protection. Great grandma from down south had carved it by hand, sculpting magical symbols and the frightening faces of supernatural creatures into the molding. Each character had a different personality. But they never scared her. They were monsters, but they were her friends. She would talk to them when she was little. And sometimes they talked back.

But the glass itself was even more mysterious, undercoated with some strange metallic material even antique dealers couldn't positively identify. It was not sheer and totally flat; it had a sight waviness and appeared more crystalline. There were tiny bubbles inside, with iridescent rainbow colors growing like smudges along its edges. It seemed to be discernibly deeper than a regular mirror, not like the modern mass-produced ones over your bathroom sink. Cloudier, more luminous, as if another world existed inside.

Many nights, as she watched from her bed, corporeal shadows would dance cryptic ballets. Glowing silhouettes would give enigmatic dramatic performances in the fathomless depths. She often heard sounds emanating from it. Distant murmuring voices she couldn't quite understand. Mystical chanting, joyous singing, tragic wailing.

As she grew older, the visions faded, and the voices fell silent. As if its juju was meant only for the very young. Toddlers who still thought enchantments were real and life might turn out as joyously as a fairy tale. The further she was forced into school and books and the reality of everyday existence, the more distant the creatures became, until they were stored away in her memory as childish things best to be forgotten. Couldn't be telling friends from the neighborhood about ghosts haunting your bedroom or you'd be forever banished between the nerd and geek sections of your class.

Until that devastating day her mother ceased to be. That was also the day her childhood ended. No more fun and games. No more playdates with other kids or sleepovers at cousin's houses. Because Cassie was now forced to live with her dad. And everyone in the hood knew he was bad news. Her mama hadn't heard a word or seen a penny from him since the divorce.

The wake and funeral were a blur of hugs and kisses from people she hardly knew, all dressed in their Sunday best. She was expected to meet and greet all these creepy strangers who pinched her cheeks and told her how much she'd grown. What sickened

Cassie was -- they were having fun, telling old stories, and laughing with each other like it was some kind of party. How could they joke around at such a solemn event?

After enduring a few hours of this torture, she had to escape. Her only way of coping was to hide out in a quiet corner of the funeral home and avoid all the fuss. To close her eyes and pretend her mom didn't really die, that this was all just a bad dream. Then having the painful truth storm back into her mind and ruin her fantasy.

She sobbed to herself as quietly as she could, hoping nobody would find her and drag her back to that dreaded coffin. Seeing her mother's beautiful face trapped in that waxy effigy of lifelessness was too unbearable. Her vitality had vanished without a trace, and that was what made her who she was. This stiff husk of once human flesh was not her mother, it was just a scarecrow reminder that she was gone forever.

Her dad didn't cause much of a fuss at the services. He really seemed angry that he had to even be there at all. And the whole social services nightmare was a garbled litany of legal nonsense to poor Cassie. She was treated like a ragdoll, arms stretched this way and that, as her mom's relatives tried in vain to keep her away from her father. But the laws were the laws.

When he first saw Cassie again, she wore a dress for a developing young lady, not the little baby he remembered. He looked down at her strangely, not the way a father should stare at his own flesh and blood. She realized that she was starting to become a woman, that he was noticing her body. Said she was starting to look just like her mama. He forced himself uncomfortably close, cornering her in the lobby. Cassie began to get scared and started to whimper.

He stormed off in a rage. Cassie stayed with her auntie that night.

The next morning was shiny and sizzling hot, like the stainless-steel pan Aunt Thelma scrambled her eggs and bacon in. The kind of day Mom lived for. Breakfast was delicious, yet Cassie just shoved it around on her plate. Until she spotted her daddy pull up outside in his dented purple beater. Realizing this would probably be her last decent meal for a long while, she wolfed it down.

There was more hollering and threats at the front door, but Cassie ended up going off with her dad. First stop was her mom's apartment to pick up her things. Her dad could never afford the rent for such a nice apartment in that area. As soon as he entered the front door, she could see the madness in his face. He wasn't just angry at the world; he was insanely jealous of it. Just seeing all her mom's pretty things caused his inner rage to explode.

"Look at all this bullshit," he sneered. Without a sentient thought of how much money he could get for it, he kicked her antique rocking chair and sent it smashing into the wall. With a swipe of his arm, he sent all her China cups and saucers crashing to the hardwood floor, oblivious to their worth on the internet.

Then he saw the dolls. Whatever hatred which still lingered inside over his former wife erupted. He strangled them, tore off their clothes, ripped off their arm and legs, beat them against the walls, twisted their heads off. He either didn't notice or simply didn't care that Cassie was bawling her eyes out at his rampage.

"Daddy, please. You can sell this stuff, make some money," she cried out.

Nothing can stop a crackhead on a crazy spree like the word money. It's like a magic spell which can stop them in their tracks faster than a charging rhino getting hit with a tranquilizing dart.

Instantly, he was on his cellphone jabbering to some losers. Talking about trading the wonderful things mom had spent a lifetime collecting for a few little white rocks which would poof into smoke and disappear in one night.

In less time than Dominos could deliver a pizza, two creeps showed up and started hauling it all off. Stripped the place bare. Furniture, appliances, even got on a stepstool and pry-barred away the antique crown molding from along the ceiling.

When they got to Cassie's room, she kept silent, realizing there was no reasoning with these addicts. Her TV and all her other things were as good as gone. Trying her best to emulate her mother, she thought quickly and formulated a plan. Cassie knew that he was still her father and was counting on that single tiny thread of decency she hoped still remained. When they got to her prized possession, that's when she let him have it.

"Please Daddy, not that. Please let me keep the mirror, please, please."

She got down on her hands and knees, clawing at the legs of his filthy jeans, pleading to keep just one thing to remind her of the life she spent here. His eyes shifted sideways; his lips curled. She had struck that faint chord of humanity he had kept so closely guarded his entire life. His face twisted as he peered down at her. Even though his homeless pals were begging him to sell it, she had hit the bullseye.

"Keep that piece of shit. Ain't worth my trouble anyways."

Big mistake. Huge.

Cassie was numb as she was shoved into her dad's car and driven away from her mom's home for the last time. Didn't even care about how dirty the inside of the window was. She leaned her cheek against it and let the tears flow like the last waning raindrops of a terrible thunderstorm. They trickled down the glass, leaving clean little rivulets through the dust. She watched as the two losers drove a rusted white box truck filled with her mother's memories off to the junk dealer. She knew she would cry and cry about this moment for the rest of her life. But for now, she was drained of every last ounce of emotion.

Her father's apartment was worse than she had ever imagined. Potholes in the flooring, craters in the drywall. A mountain of dirty dishes in the kitchen sink that had been piled up so long, green mold was growing around the edges of the pots and pans. Rats and roaches coexisted in their own little ecosystem.

She was shoved into a small, dank closet which seemed like an old pantry. A string hung from the ceiling to turn the single cobwebbed light bulb on and off. A vile mattress had been tossed over some stacked up milk crates. This was to be her bedroom. How DCFS let this poor fragile girl be forced to live there was an indictment of the entire welfare system.

Cassie feared for her life that night, and not because of the teeming wildlife. Dad's two buddies returned, and soon, the faint smell of burning rubber and nail polish remover wafted under her door. She knew they were smoking crack.

But she made sure to carry her mirror inside. It was more important to her than the duffel bag of clothes her dad had stuffed, or her toothbrush and hairbrush. She wasn't about to ask them for help. Searching the chipped and faded green walls, Cassie found an old nail which must have been used to hold up a picture frame once upon a time.

It was a mighty struggle, but somehow, she stretched the wire from the back of the mirror to the nail on the wall, and let it slide into place. Didn't take more than one slight shift to make it perfectly straight. How much safer she felt, having it defending her bedside, those little carved wooden creatures standing guard like monstrous little soldiers.

The next few days were spent hiding in her closet, only sneaking out to use the bathroom or get a sip of water. She refused to even use a glass, just stuck her head under the faucet and caught water into her mouth as it poured out. Tasted rusty. Cassie knew once the crack was gone, her father's temper would return, so she stayed out of his way. Didn't even beg for an Egg McMuffin.

But eventually they had to bump into each other. All Cassie had for bedtime was a short Minnie Mouse t-shirt nightie. Dad watched her with predatory eyes. He was having a hard time controlling himself. She shut her door before lying down, but as soon as he thought she had fallen asleep, he cracked it open and peered inside. She squinted her eyes shut so he would think she was unconscious, but she could sense him hovering out there, watching her. Puffing cigarettes, pacing back and forth.

Then he stormed out of the house, leaving her alone for hours. She had just drifted off when he finally returned, making a clamor only a man could make in such a barren apartment. Whether it was courage or curiosity, Cassie peeked out her door to assess what kind of danger she was in. He appeared disheveled, almost panic-stricken, tearing off his clothes and washing his hands and face over and over.

As he dried himself with the used shirt he had just peeled off, once again, his inner GPS recentered back to Cassie. She silently laid back down as he soft-pedaled over and stood at her bedside, glaring down at her, smelling of cheap wine and crack pipes. She pretended to be napping yet felt this evil aura emanating from him. She had to keep silent, but her instincts inside were screaming that she wasn't safe, that he was just about to grab her. Do horrible things to her.

But then, at the last instant, he spun around and bustled out of her pantry in anger. Cassie cracked open one eye as he left, just to make sure he was truly going.

Just as her father passed the precious mirror, he twitched spastically. He whipped his hand back as if swatting at a yellow jacket swarming around his head. Cassie had seen behavior like this before from junkies in the streets. Yet this was a little different. He stumbled out as if frightened of something.

Yet the face she saw reflected in the glass as he passed by was not her father's. It was the ghostly visage of a tortured young woman, silently shrieking in terror.

Cassie freaked out, but stifled the scream with her pillow so her dad wouldn't hear. He slammed the door shut as he left, so the whole rattrap was pitch black again. The image's faint whimpering began to grow louder, pulsating through the very air she was breathing. Eerie, otherworldly. The stuff of nightmares.

But Cassie could sense these wails weren't hostile. The vibrations Cassie felt from this entity were not threatening. They were moans of sadness and pain. The despair of having her young life cut short. The sting of knowing she would never taste another meal, never touch another loved one, never celebrate another year of life. A bleakness which brought tears to Cassie's own eyes.

"Hello?" she tried to communicate, waving her hand at the sad wraith floating in the wooden frame. The only reply was an awful weeping which reverberated in the wall where the mirror hung.

Every few minutes, her bruised and bloodied profile would reappear as an ethereal glimmer. It lit up the tiny space as if faint candlelight from another dimension. She was a stranger, of that Cassie was certain, yet resembled someone she had seen before, maybe at a restaurant or grocery store. Not exactly a sweet person, more hardened from a rough life. But still worthy of decency, of a shoulder to cry on.

Cassie asked what had happened to her, which caused her to cry out even harder. Long fake nails scratched downwards across her bruised and bloodied cheeks. She attempted to tell her story, only to have the hysterical sounds spilling from her lips come out as garbled moans. Her pain was so tangible, Cassie felt her own heart breaking. She had to soothe this spirit's torture somehow.

Even though the conversation was completely one-sided, Cassie began to whisper to the lonely visage. She spoke for hours, blurting out whatever things a 13-year-old girl could think of to comfort a living corpse. It seemed to work, as the whimpering started to dissipate. As dawn approached, the lamenting finally ceased; and Cassie finally drifted off to an uneasy sleep.

The morning brought sunshine creeping through scratches in the pantry window, which had been spray painted black to avoid paying for a new curtain. But it brought no solace to Cassie. Nothing to cheer her up or reassure her that life would somehow turn around. That she would soon be happy again. The mirror was silent, as was the rest of the house, so she felt safe for the moment.

But she was her mother's daughter and didn't have that sit around and mope kind of attitude when things got bad. Her mom always told her that everybody has their own mountain of troubles. But you can't neglect them, or they'll keep growing until they're so massive they're impossible to conquer. The secret was to tear it down one molehill at a time. And this dump wasn't going to clean itself. She hopped out of bed and got down to work.

Cassie kissed her fingers, touched them softly to the mirror, and said "Good morning." There was no trace of the spirit which had haunted it the night before, but she knew it was still in there and needed someone to console her. Then she headed to the kitchen. Under the sink she found several bottles of cleaning products, nearly full, and a pair of yellow rubber gloves still sealed in plastic wrapping. She wiped down all the kitchen counters and inside the cupboards several times and laid clean paper towels over them.

Then she tackled Mount Filthpile. Scrubbed every single plate, mug, and spoon clean as the proverbial whistle, placing them neatly out to dry. That stinky sink was the main attraction for all the critters in this ex-con condominium, and she grimaced through the whole ordeal. Although it was obvious that they were only scattering off to hide inside the walls, at least they weren't crawling around everywhere like they owned the place.

Found some blankets and bed sheets in a cabinet and tossed them in the washing machine. Prayed as she turned the knob to start her up. But it worked perfectly, as if it had barely ever been used. A glance at her phone told her she had already been working for six hours, but there was still her own tiny cubicle to wash down. She dragged out the bed and milk crates, then washed and rewashed the walls and floors, turning three buckets of sparkling clean water into gray, polluted bilge before they stopped resisting and allowed themselves to be sanitized.

With her father still not home, she noticed he slept on a single mattress himself, and it was practically new. With the sneaky smile of a young girl trying to trick her old man, she switched her nasty ass one for his. Covered it with clean sheets, pillowcases and a blanket, hoping the fresh smell would cover up her thievery. Then dragged his new one into her own little corner of hell. At least this pigsty would be a little more livable after she was done.

Her anxiety ran high as she waited for her father to get home. He was so erratic; she could never be certain of how he would react to anything. He arrived happily plastered after a bout of day-drinking with his fellow unemployed clowns. To her surprise, he was so impressed that he gave her five dollars to go get herself a sandwich. Those were slave wages even in China, let alone America, but she convinced herself that everything was going to work itself out.

Cassie had been texting back and forth with a cousin who lived ninety miles away. He told her she could live in his attic apartment rent-free until she turned eighteen and was legally an adult. As long as her dad could keep cashing the public aid checks he was getting for housing and feeding her, she doubted he would even care that she was missing.

There was only one thing holding her back. Cassie needed to find someone to pick her up and drive her there. The cousin didn't trust his car except for a few miles to work or the grocery store. He truly wanted to help, but he couldn't risk his only mode of transportation. The rest of the family was still boohooing about her situation, but no one had the guts to cross her father.

Things simmered down for a while, but after just a few days, angry dad reemerged. Watched her do housework with a perversity he didn't even attempt to conceal. Touched and kissed her in ways that were more than inappropriate. Caught him sniffing her used underwear that she left near the washing machine between cycles. She knew she had to make a move sooner than later.

The floor was so creaky, Cassie could always hear him loitering outside her room. Every night as she slept, he snuck inside and stood over her, practically drooling like the Big Bad Wolf in an old cartoon. She could sense what he was thinking, wanting to do things she had to force herself not to imagine. Every time he did, the ghost girl in the mirror began to stir up. Her moaning echoed; her glowing face reappeared on the glass, almost as a warning.

None of the supernatural stuff seemed to register in her father's vacuous skull, only made him uneasy, gave him the jitters. Just as Cassie thought he was about to assault her, her spooky friend bawled out a blood-curdling shriek. And her dad's face twisted up, as if he felt a sharp pain in his conscience. His shoulders hunched and he glanced around like the cops were sneaking up on him while he was buying drugs. He finally couldn't stand it anymore, and raced out of the house like ghosts were after him.

And actually, one really was.

"Thank you," Cassie murmured softly. It was easy for the imaginative part of her young brain to believe that there was a ghost in the mirror. But it was still quite difficult for the older, more practical section to accept. At least the spirit had frightened him off, and she was safe for a few hours. She played video games and texted back and forth with friends on her phone until loud slamming of the back door signaled his return.

He marched straight to her bed, looming over her once more, sweating, wild-eyed, almost like "See what you made me do?"

Just like the last time, as he stormed off, he lashed his arms out as if swatting away his personal demons. And again, as he left, it wasn't her father's reflection paralleled in the mirror, but a young woman's. A completely different one. Another phantom haunting the glass, beaten even more savagely than the first. She sobbed and cursed at him. Even though her words were imperceptible, Cassie could tell foul language when she heard it. She was in agony, and as mad as hell at her father. He must have done horrible things to her, crimes that only a sicko could dream up.

Why didn't her dad's face ever appear in the family heirloom? Only tragic girls sobbing over their own deaths? Was it somehow refusing his evil countenance? Cassie kept trying to communicate with these women, but everything they said sounded muddled, distorted. As if the barrier between their world and Cassie's was too distant, too impregnable.

Paranormal problems like these would be rough for even the most mature adult to handle. Kids her age still haven't developed all the reasoning and solid judgement that someone in their twenties or thirties take for granted. Cassie felt imprisoned in her disgusting little prison cell, but still did her best to comfort the agitated spirits she lived with. And at the same time, try to keep her menacing wolf of a father at bay.

This behavior continued for weeks. Every few days, he would lurk over Cassie's frail form as she feigned slumber. Shoving his hands into his pockets to avoid doing something unforgivable to his only child. It was clear he wanted to do things that no normal father would ever even consider, but something was preventing him from doing it.

Was it his conscience, or were the ancient specters which had been lurking for generations inside the glass protecting her? Maybe it didn't matter. He would race out with a scowl, then return hours later. And once again, a new spirit would light from his stress-mangled shoulders to find refuge in the glass.

Cassie was desperate to put an end to the horrible crimes her father was committing. But what could she tell people? That some ghosts wanted to file charges? Who would believe her without some kind of proof?

Finally, the fifth time he stormed out that way, he came back alone. No new victim had clung to her dad's shoulders back to the apartment that night. He was even more agitated than ever before, calling his creepy friends back and forth. His voice was so different. Frightened scowls, spoken so softly she couldn't understand them. But Cassie could sense what was at the heart of these furious back-and-forths.

Something had gone wrong. Whatever perverted felonies he had committed that night did not go as planned. He was scared shitless. Trying to beg friends for help with alibis to confirm his whereabouts.

"Tell them I was with you," were the only words she could hear clearly, over and over.

It was strange, because he never even came into her room. There were now four young ladies in the mirror, and they raged around the glass with an anxiousness Cassie had never seen in them before. Whatever had occurred, it seemed they somehow knew the details. They all wailed in harmony, beckoning out into the darkness. But this time, their voices were not mournful cries. They were enchanting songs. Sirens begging for some lost soul to come join them.

Suddenly, Cassie felt a different presence approaching. A brutal tempest, an energy so furious that its volatile wake entered her room before it did.

Her father.

He charged towards her cubbyhole and kicked the door open so viciously that splinters from the frame pelted the bed. His expression was so enraged, it was like an anatomical map of anger on a human face.

"Stop that shit. Shut up. Shut the hell up," he screamed at poor Cassie.

"But, Daddy, I'm not making a sound."

He staggered back, huffs and puffs stammering out as if he had been drowning in his own emotions and couldn't catch his breath. His head reeled after he scoped out her little cubby hole and realized he must be imagining it all. The siren choir kept singing their angry gospel, and now he could still hear it. He squeezed his temples with his fingertips in a desperate attempt to force his brain to make sense of what was happening. Then he covered his ears, trying to silence the ghostly tinnitus which was haunting him closer and closer to lunacy.

Unable to cope with his crippled sanity, he launched himself back out of the apartment, babbling incoherently to drown out the song of those vengeful harpies. Didn't even bother to close the door behind him.

Cassie trembled, realizing how close he had come to assaulting her. She thought the craziest part of the night was over, but things were just getting started. Just as she settled down back under the blankets, a strange light began to stream through the blacked-out window. It was the middle of the night, yet this intense glow kept getting brighter and brighter.

Suddenly, a form slowly began to emerge through the solid glass, a slow-motion entrance so enchanting that Cassie involuntarily stopped breathing. First a nose, then eyes, cheeks, ears. It was a face of a once-angelic woman, now battered and bruised. Her body followed, naked and ethereal. She floated right over Cassie, who lay transfixed on her bed. She wanted to reach up and touch it, but the chill of this otherworldly presence forced her to remain shuddering beneath the blankets.

The lady melted straight into the mirror, where she was immediately welcomed by the other victims, who swarmed around her with love and empathy. Cassie was so frozen in fear, she almost wet the sheets. The voices inside the glass now changed from moans to greetings. Now five faces swirled back and forth in the depths, all distorted with gore and misery.

"Hello, new lady," Cassie murmured, greeting the newest addition as she did with all the other girls. But this one had a surprise in store for her.

"Hello? Where are you? Who are you?" the specter replied.

"You can hear me? You understand?"

"Yeah, I hear ya. Where the hell am I? Everything is so blurry and foggy."

"You're not going to like what I have to tell you."

"Clue me in, little bish," the spirit called out with a voice sweet as honey.

"You're dead. Someone killed you."

"Bullshit. You're crazy."

"Please, try to talk to the other girls in there. They can explain it all to you better than I can."

The spirit murmured, then took flight, retreating into the deep recesses of the mirror, where the other souls were gathered together. A haunting symphony of emotional warbles echoed from inside, the ghosts conversing with frightening inflections. As the discussions became more heated, the glass bubbled out like a cauldron, a maelstrom of supernatural activity boiling out of control. Cassie quickly pulled away, thinking the ectoplasm might be dangerous.

It seemed that trying to make dead folks accept they were

ghosts was no easy task. Cassie tried her best to listen along, as the five ladies went back and forth. There was a lot of anger and denial at first, followed by tears and anguish. She learned that this new woman's name was Jasmine, and she was a manicurist at the local beauty salon, just three blocks from her dad's place. She was walking home from BJ's Bar down the street when a guy came out of nowhere and coldcocked her on the side of the head.

Momentarily dazed, he was able to drag her into an abandoned storefront. He punched her a few more times to make sure she stayed dazed and confused, then began to rape her. But Jasmine recovered more quickly than he expected and kicked him off. Frustrated and angry, he whipped out a switchblade that looked like a foot long. Jasmine realized he was about to murder her right there. She grabbed at his arm, and they struggled across the vacant sales floor, crashing into dusty furniture. But her pants had been pulled down around her ankles, and she tripped to the hardwood floor.

He seized the upper hand, holding her down with his free hand, but she rolled her body around, so she wasn't an easy target. Jasmine scratched his face like a cornered wildcat, but he still managed to bury his blade deeply into her chest. She must have caught his eye with her nail because he screamed and let her go. She dragged herself up to her feet and ran until she couldn't take another step, finally dropping to the sidewalk. She told her story to some people who tried to console her, then she bled out. As she breathed her last, she said she felt herself float up from her own body. Then supernatural forces led her here.

Through Jasmine, Cassie finally learned the identities of the other lost souls haunting her little world.

Denise, the first victim, was another crackhead like her father. She remembered partying with some guys until all of them left but one. Then that bastard couldn't control himself. Raped and stabbed her to death.

The second was Alice, an accountant, who was just in the wrong place at the wrong time. Her car had stalled on the way home from a party, and some guy she had never seen before offered to help. She suffered the same fate.

Then Carla got off the Greyhound from out of town and was walking towards her girlfriend's house. They were going to spend a nice weekend together, but it wasn't to be.

And Josie, who worked the late shift at UPS unloading trucks. She was so tired that she couldn't even put up much of a fight.

None of them had any clue about what happened to their bodies after they were murdered. Jasmine said her poor, tortured glassmates were all a little insane. Being slaughtered and trapped in some spirit world would probably take a mental toll on even the toughest folks.

Cassie felt a strange sense of relief that she could finally communicate with one of them. It made her realize how frightened she had been having these otherworldly entities sharing her tiny pantry. The turmoil surrounding her mother's passing was terrible enough for a young lady. Having Jasmine to talk to seemed to take a huge weight off her tiny shoulders.

They whispered to each other for hours, until Cassie drifted off to Neverland.

The next day, Cassie decided to creep out of her closet and watch the TV in the living room. She liked it because the screen was so much larger than her Android phone, even though there were so many commercials. Out of nowhere, Jasmine's face popped up on the news. Reporters said she had been found still alive just a few blocks away, raped and stabbed, yet somehow escaped her attacker. With her dying breaths, she was able to tell the witnesses who found her that she scratched his face and ran away before he could finish the job.

Her dad still had fresh scratches on his face. He looked away from her, blushing harder as the segment continued. Sweat was visibly bubbling up on his balding forehead. She stared at him while they watched. Cassie was now certain that everything Jasmine had told her was true. When he finally built up the courage to look at his daughter, he could see his own guilt reflected in her eyes.

Cassie saw a deluge of emotions raging inside him. Fury over letting his latest victim escape. Fear over the growing chances of getting caught. Terror over the thought of possibly having to kill his new meal ticket so she wouldn't snitch to the cops. It all welled up inside his selfish little mind until he exploded.

He bolted up from his flea market lounge chair and kicked the TV, shattering the screen, then stormed out of the room as it toppled over. On his way out, he punched another hole in the shabby drywall. He tried that at her mother's apartment once, not realizing it was solid plaster. Busted his hand up so badly, he was in a cast and sling for weeks.

Cassie sprinted to her cubbyhole and slammed the door shut, her short breaths racing with her rapid heartbeats. Curling up into a ball in the corner of her makeshift bed under the covers, silently praying for the spirits in the mirror to protect her. She basically trembled herself to sleep that night.

It didn't seem possible, but she woke up in even worse shape the next morning. The terror of walking out to face her father combined with kidneys ready to burst from desperately having to pee. She had no choice but to leave her flimsy saferoom or else wet the bed.

But he was gone, only leaving the faint smell of burnt rocks to haunt her nostrils. Cassie knew she had to tell someone about the murders but didn't want to go to the police. Cops in this neighborhood had no time for the rantings of a teenaged girl. Unless she was selling Girl Scout Cookies.

She set her sights on Miss Kwan, her homeroom teacher. A sweet 25-year-old, just starting her career. All she wanted to do was help kids grow up with a sense of wonder. Teach them that learning new stuff was a lot cooler than they might think.

Cassie waited until lunch, then, while all the other kids ran out for recess, she attempted to approach her. She stumbled towards her, then retreated back to her desk. After repeating this several times, Miss Kwan finally had enough.

"What is it, Cassie? Did your computer get stolen again?"

"I wish it was something that simple."

Now Miss Kwan was intrigued. She snapped her laptop shut and gave the nervous girl her undivided attention.

"What is it? You can tell me anything."

"I…uh…well my…umm," Cassie couldn't force the words out of her mouth.

"I won't judge you, if that's what you're worried about," she said.

"Okay, here goes. I think my dad is the one who is killing all those poor ladies."

The color on Miss Kwan's face drained pale as she fought to

stop her jaw from dropping. Maybe she thought this was all about who had broken the microscope or let the guinea pig escape. Basic school mischief. This was quite the bombshell.

"Come closer. Speak very softly. I don't want anyone else to eavesdrop," she said.

She quietly closed the classroom door and sat Cassie down in her own teacher's chair. Made sure she knew that she was treating this with the utmost importance and secrecy.

Leaving out all the paranormal parts of the story, Cassie explained every detail that made her father look guilty. From running out on the nights of each of the murders, to the scratches on his face, to the weird ways he had been touching her.

Miss Kwan kneeled in front of Cassie, an honestly concerned expression resonating on her face. There was no doubt she believed Cassie's story.

"I'm going to investigate whatever I can without getting too close," Miss Kwan assured her. "If I can prove any part of what you're saying is true, I'm going straight to the police. Is that alright with you?"

The tears welling up in Cassie's eyes finally exploded into a full-blown crying jag. She collapsed into Miss Kwan's arms, and her teacher gave her that heartfelt hug she'd been longing for since her mama died. Not a "I'm so sorry" hug, but a "I really care about you and will do anything I can to help you" type embrace.

They bawled until the tears ran dry, and as they pulled away, Miss Kwan shared her box of Kleenex. Only two were left, but they made it work, giggling a bit as they tossed the soggy tissues into the trash can under her desk.

Cassie kept going in for more hugs. It felt so good after

suffering with the cold shoulder her father always had for her. She felt so bad when her little wet nose dripped onto Miss Kwan's blouse, but a cute little wink and smile told her she didn't mind.

Cassie never made it outside for lunch. She floated back to her desk and slumped into the awkwardly attached chair. As she exhaled, she felt most of the fear and nervous energy which had been building up inside her for weeks swarm out of her body, a cloud of tension evaporating before her very eyes. Finally revealing her deep, dark secrets expelled all the guilt and remorse she had been feeling like some evil spirit which had possessed her. Isn't it strange how decent people feel ashamed and responsible for someone else's crimes while they themselves experience nothing but narcissistic bliss?

A heat wave invaded the area by the next morning. When Cassie crept into the back door of her dad's place after school, the stale air was so stifling she could hardly breathe. The refrigerator wasn't humming, the air conditioner wasn't blowing, the fan refused to turn. Obviously paying electric bills wasn't as high on her father's list of priorities as just getting high. She dropped her things off onto her bed and scampered back outside.

When she turned the corner to the front of the building, she saw a mini-waterpark had unexpectedly come to town. Someone had unscrewed the fire hydrant just enough to let the water shoot out like a sideways geyser. Kids and teens were jumping in and out of this pressurized fountain, giggling happily. Cassie was about to join in when she spotted her father on their front stoop, gazing at all of them in bathing suits the way a wolf stared at lambs straying from the flock.

Instead, she found a shady spot a hundred feet away where a tree had blocked off most of the sun's heat and sat on the curb. She only took off her shoes and socks, dipping her feet into the tiny flood of chilly water streaming along towards the sewer. Enough of a breeze blew in from the lakefront to make the weather bearable.

Just watching everyone else enjoy themselves brought a smile to her face, even though she really couldn't participate. It brought back memories of how happy her grandma would get watching kids playing in the park near her mom's place. Cassie almost felt content for a moment. But then it all went wrong. Miss Kwan was suddenly at her dad's porch, talking to him. That tension which had all but disappeared returned to stab Cassie right in the spine, actually jerking her into a distressing posture.

"No, no, no, no," kept repeating in her brain. Why would she come here? Didn't she realize how dangerous it would be for her to confront this predator? And how dangerous it would be for Cassie? Why did it seem like some of the smartest people can make some of the dumbest mistakes? There was definitely a glaring difference between school smarts and street smarts in action.

There was a quick, heated confrontation. A few hostile gestures from her father, and Miss Kwan was gone. Cassie thought she saw her return to her car and drive away, but in her muddled mind, nothing was distinctively clear. All she could think about was whether she should run as far and as fast as she could and never look back or go back into that vile flophouse and hope to survive the night.

She crept from the curb and hid under the entranceway inlet of a grocery store where her father had no chance to spot her. She waited for the longest time. Cops and firemen came by with a big, strange wrench and turned off the good times, to the dismay of the crowd. With the gusher gone, they all wandered back home a couple at a time. Only a drizzle of dirty water trickled along the pavement when her father finally walked off, destination unknown.

Sneaking around back, Cassie tiptoed in through the back door and rushed straight to her bedroom, closing the door as silently as possible even though she knew he wasn't there. She tried to think of ways to barricade it so he couldn't get in, but figured any type of resistance would only make him more pissed off than he already was. The ghosts in the glass were suspiciously quiet, so she tried her best to get some rest for the upcoming storm she knew would erupt the minute he got back.

And sure enough, hours later, her pantry door busted open. There he was, looming over her again, even more angry than ever. She saw bulging, ferocious eyes, quivering lips, menacing hands, his entire body shaking with rage. Cassie instinctively jammed her back against the far wall, but she was trapped. Tears and pleading were useless. Nothing could prevent him from doing anything he wanted to her. Her thoughts spontaneously flashed into prayer, begging for a quick, merciful death, not to suffer hours of perverted torture.

He snatched her up to his face and shook her so violently that her neck throbbed from the jerking motion.

"You're my flesh and blood! How could you do that to me? I'm gonna send you where your Mama is."

Cassie realized this was the end. She let herself go, releasing her mind and body to Fate, hoping that somehow distancing her brain from this torture would make it less horrible. Her life had been miserable since her father took it over, so maybe it was all for the best. Suffer through these last agonizing moments in order to rejoin her mother in heaven. She curls into a ball and awaits whatever evil he had in store.

But as he is about to end her existence, Cassie sees Miss Kwan materialize above his hunched shoulders, bruised and sobbing. He had murdered her, and her spirit had tagged along just as all the others had. She joined inside the mirror with Jasmine and the others. The looking glass trembled and quaked, banging against the wall, trying to work its way free from the wire holding it back.

And then… CRASH! It shattered mightily over the back of her father's head. His expression was one of pure shock.

At that instant, time decelerated, as if all of the magic in the mirror had broken free, escaping to do what it had always been meant to. Protect Cassie.

Her father's face slow motioned into a grimace. All the different shards twirled in the air like in a dream. Spinning in a seemingly choreographed dance around his skull. Each large chunk showed a different face. Miss Kwan, Jasmine, and all the rest flicker on their own separate pieces as they slowly swirled downwards, energized by the hatred of each towards their killer. They should have all fallen harmlessly to the floor, but instead begin to move in tandem, a haunting mobile of crystalline effigies dancing in the air from invisible strings.

Cassie was mesmerized. They were so beautiful, scintillating in the darkness surrounding her would-be killer. Dad was frozen in fear, a statue of fear and horror which would have been perfect in some museum of the bizarre. That split second was burned into Cassie's memory forever. As what happened next, when each individual shard buried themselves into his shoulders, head, face, and back. Each victim screamed with vengeance as they sank themselves deep into this monster's flesh. Their shrieking hurts Cassie's ears. The girls twisted their shards to inflict agony on their murderer. He dropped to his knees, wailing in pain and begging for mercy.

But the glass has no pity. Blood spurted all over her cubbyhole, even across Cassie's face. He writhed on the floor, gasping his last breaths, face longing for Cassie to forgive him. He grasps up at Cassie with eyes begging for pity. And even after all the unforgivable things he had done, all the unspeakable crimes he had committed, she still felt sympathy. The kind of misguided consolation that only a daughter who still loved her Daddy could understand.

She reached out to him, one last tortuous appeal for his love. But it was just a ploy. All of it was just an act. He turned vicious again, whipping out a huge blade from his back pocket, as shiny as the shards yet still stained with Miss Kwan's blood. He took a diving leap, slashing out to kill her. He could never control the evil inside himself. He was a narcissistic piece of trash who never deserved any empathy.

Just as he is about to stab her, the huge piece of glass with Miss Kwan's face on it slashed across the room, slicing his throat wide open from ear to ear.

His head hit the floor before his body.

A few weeks later, Cassie is sitting in her new bedroom at her Aunt Thelma's house. Not as nice as her mom's place, but light-years away from the horrors of her father's dump.

The doorbell rang and her auntie answered it. She can hear that it's the police, even though she's busy and not really paying attention. Something about finding five bodies of young women in a vacant lot. All different races and nationalities, just like her mother's dolls. Raped, murdered and buried in shallow graves in a vacant lot behind some thick bushes near her school. Cassie knew exactly where that spot was. She used to have to sit in the car and wait while her father checked into a crack house nearby.

They say there was a new hole that had been dug, one so small it could only have fit a 12-year-old kid. He must have been planning to kill Cassie, so the self-defense theory of her father's killing was valid. Although how she cut his entire head off with a piece of glass was puzzling. Especially with no cuts on her own hands.

But none of that concerned Cassie anymore. She had been saved, protected by the magic mirror. And now she had to return the favor. She was busy Krazy-Gluing all the big shards together, recreating her savior. It was already mostly pieced together except for tiny slivers she was now painstakingly adding on. As she finished, the entire surface began to shimmer. And then it healed itself, filling in all the missing fragments and smoothing out all the cracks until it looked just as it had before.

She wondered why it didn't guard her beloved mom from her abusers. Maybe it could only strike out in matters of life or death. Maybe it skipped a generation. She was too traumatized to give it much thought. Later on, when she had time to grow and distance herself from this terror and heartache, maybe then she would figure it all out. For now, she spent her days trying to heal her wounded soul. And make sure this heirloom stayed in the family. Someday, one of her own children or grandchildren might need it.

Cassie stared into it. Deep inside, in the cloudy distance beyond the reflections, she could see her father being chased and tormented by the old demons in the glass.

Her great grandma would be mighty proud of her.

(He almost seemed to be transforming into a monster himself.

Perhaps that's who these creatures were. Once evil humans who spend their eternity protecting helpless victims in the hope that one day their own souls would be forgiven.)

Ditching School

Trying to rediscover your true self when tiny fragments of personality have been expunged is the most frustrating facet of a lost life. My mind functioned well, but now felt like a blackboard filled with equations that had all the answers erased. I thought I had it all together as a teenager a dozen years ago. Lettering in baseball and basketball in high school. 4.5 GPA. More scholarships than I knew what to do with. Heading to Stanford to major in cybersecurity. Dating all the hottest babes in town and rating them to my buddies like they were the Billboard Top 100. We all think we're invulnerable at that age. And so much smarter than anybody else.

Summer had ended and my senior year was just about to start. Hated autumn. Living in the Midwest, it meant the end of all the balls-out fun we had during shorts and t-shirt season. Cruising around town, showing off the 2010 Corvette convertible my parents bought me. I couldn't decide which I enjoyed more, watching all the girls swooning or the guys glaring at me with envy. Backyard pool parties with cheerleaders wasted on White Claws. Soaking wet, spilling out of their bikinis. I loved warm weather.

That's why I was so psyched to be moving to California after the school year was over. No more blizzards for me, except the Dairy Queen kind. I loved my friends and family here, but I needed to go explore who I really was when I could live on my own. No parental pressures, no buddies pushing you to get wasted. Just me and school and a whole different atmosphere. I had definite plans for my future, but you're only young once, and that's the time to go all out. Experiment. Test your limits. Leave no stone unturned. Do the things that you can't do when you're wrinkly and feeble. Make sure your future Bucket List is short. And your memories look like a PowerPoint presentation of every awesome life experience imaginable.

Two more semesters to go and I was outta here. But I was still having a blast. Halloween was closing in. Drinking Jack Daniels and apple cider out in the orchards, everyone's breath turning to steam as they exhaled. And the scary movies. Leatherface. Jason. Michael Myers. All heroes of mine. Monsters were so badass because they scared the shit out of you even though you knew they weren't real. Then you could switch to the hockey game afterwards and all the jitters dissolved.

One night all the games ended early, so we decided to take a ride to the scariest place in the county. The Lunar Ether Temple was a farm encampment about 18 miles outside the city limits. One of those weirdo cults that pretended to be Christian just to get the real Christians off their backs. So silent and distant, nobody knew who or what they actually worshipped. Developed from one of those sects of cloistered monks who had occupied the same spot for centuries. They never shaved or cut their hair, so the men looked like Rasputin. Guys wore black friar robes, women wore white. Local descriptions of their lifestyle ranged from "just a bunch of New Age hippies" to "baby murdering sickos," depending on what type of person you asked.

But no one could deny that the fruits and vegetables they grew were some of the tastiest anywhere. Even the folks who vilified them as followers of the Anti-Christ were occasionally spotted sneaking one of their apples or pears from the local farmer's market. They were just too delicious to resist. A lot of them were just jealous because their farms couldn't cultivate produce anywhere near as scrumptious. Some used the excuse that there was something buried deep in the soil there that made it extra fertile. Ancient volcanic ash. Or Satan anointing it with his unholy blessings.

The fun thing about the farm was it was supposed to be haunted. Town records and newspaper articles dating back hundreds of years told of strange goings on in that particular neck of the woods. People disappeared. Most were never seen again, but the few that did return were never the same as they once were. Kind of lost. Spooked out of their degenerated minds. Forcibly committed to the local convents or insane asylums. Great choices. Either exorcisms or straitjackets forever.

The urban legends since then said if you went there at night at the wrong time, ghosts who haunted the area would infiltrate your body and drive you insane. So, of course, kids since the 1960's have been driving up there with their mind-altering drugs of choice and wandering around. It was a rite of passage here, peer pressure to see if you were brave enough. You had to act as if you didn't believe the old wives' tales anymore. Since then, all the guys in senior year have dared each other to take the trek to the farm and see if you had the guts to walk through the grove at midnight. High school hazing.

It was a Friday night, and a full moon was rising. My buddy Alex borrowed his dad's work van, and we piled in six of our best friends for the challenge. Driving way too fast. Speeding around curves till we almost skidded off the road. Hitting the hills fast enough to lift up off the pavement as we crested the summits.

Pounding beers and tossing the cans out the windows. The skunkweed we shared started to kick in, forcing us to giggle and maybe imagine things that weren't there. It was only the wind and the speed of our vehicle, but the twisted trees seemed to bend and sway angrily as we sped past. I think we did all that crazy stuff to forget about our true destination. We were all joking around, but still felt a little apprehension as we coasted the winding route.

As we got closer, the timberland ended. That weird mist that only seems to appear at this time of year crept across the fields covered in the remnants of this year's harvest. Alex slowed down as we reached the crumbling route that was the road towards the cult barracks, partially visible in the distance. I had passed by here in the daytime dozens of times and they always looked so harmless. But that night, they were so frightening, my scrotum shriveled up. Pot paranoia had me imagining an army of evil farmer monks descending upon us with scythes and machetes, hacking at our vitals.

He silently glided our vehicle onto a grassy knoll and turned off the ignition. We polished off whatever we had left and fell out of the vehicle, stumbling like fools and laughing our asses off. Alex took the lead. He was a year older than us and had been here before. No light posts here, just moonlight to guide us along. Puddles muddied up our designer kicks. Potholes twisted our ankles. But we trudged on, all the time thinking this was just going to be a twenty-minute excursion. A brief memory that we would chuckle about at class reunions.

The closer we got, the weirder the place seemed. This bizarre vibe grew stronger and stronger as the barracks came into view. It was just around midnight, and the cult-farmers were all asleep. Oil lamps flickered in several of the windows, highlighting how deranged the buildings looked that night. Instead of being angular, they were built in odd oval shapes, with domes crowning each one. Looked kind of like Islamic temples meets Texas Chainsaw type architecture. The others were still clowning around, but I was starting to freak. I thought maybe the weed was just really sick, but the creepiness crawled up my spine like a thousand legger skittering over my feet and across the bathroom tiles at a cheap motel.

I wanted to get the hell out of there but went along with my crew. The worst mistake of my life. A steady beat pumped at the bottom of my feet. Like a massive heartbeat was actually lifting the ground ever so slightly, then letting it settle back down every minute or so. I guess I was the only guy who noticed, because the others were just punching and shoving each other and having the times of their lives. Who could foresee that this was the turning point for mine?

I was about to ask everyone to turn back, when suddenly, huge spotlights flashed on from the sides of the buildings. We were temporarily blinded. A cruel voice blared over loudspeakers.

"This is private property. You are trespassing. Turn around and leave immediately."

Didn't need to tell me twice. We all jumped back like a pack of Rottweilers were attacking. Pounding pavement as fast as we could back to the van. I tripped a little and wavered off the road. Figured I could take a short cut through the field and get to the knoll even faster. Alex and the others were still busting a gut as they fled the scene. But just like that, they vanished. Everything went black. I couldn't see anything. Felt the earth pulled out from under me, as if the ground was a rug and someone was yanking my chain.

But they didn't disappear. I did. I had fallen through some kind of strange aperture in the dirt. Slid twenty feet straight down a greasy tunnel as fast as gravity could take me. My glasses flew off. I always felt kind of badass. I was tall, strong, and beefy for a kid my age. Smart, quick on my feet, could beat anyone in an argument. My one weakness was my vision. Practically blind without my specs. Couldn't stand contact lenses. They were too hard to put in. Hated sticking my fingers in my eyes. Always told myself I had to overcome that. Face your fear. Always put in on the back burner. I was 17 years old. Thought I would have more time.

But now it all came back to haunt me. I was trapped in a tight, mucky cave, and my visual perception was close to nil. Then I realized the palpitations I was feeling were a hundred times stronger down here. Something felt alive all around me. Everywhere. It's flesh was a nauseating pinkish color. And I was ensnared in the middle of it all. I tried desperately to climb back up, but everything was coated in slime. Gross bilge lined whatever this hell I was tangled up in. Then the worst part happened. It started to move. As if it realized I was down there. I felt like a baby inside a womb. A penis inside a vagina.

The pumping became more vigorous. This disgusting pit I had fallen into got tighter and tighter. I squirmed frantically, arms and legs struggling to escape, but I was completely enmeshed in this thing. The smell was horrific. A combination of all the worst odors of an outhouse. Piss, shit, vomit, all so overwhelming it made me regurgitate all those beers and the tacos I ate earlier. Through my blurred vision, I thought I saw the thing absorb my puke through its pores. Out of nowhere, a putrid tentacle appeared and swiped whatever I had remaining off my quivering lips. I always thought I was a badass, but I screamed like a little girl right then.

My body trembled as if I just took the Polar Plunge. Hollered as loudly as possible for my friends to come save me till my throat went raw. But the sounds reverberated back to me, muffled, as if I was in a soundproof room. This monstrous creature engulfed me completely. Its mucous covered skin was like nothing I had ever felt. A mixture of hot, melted wax and Silly Putty. I tried to punch my way out, but I was like Jonah in the belly of the whale. It began to drag me towards a different part of its anatomy. Felt veiny, as if arteries pumped in all directions. It's muscles contorted to move me along, then swarmed and entwined around my torso, squeezing at my guts so tightly I lost my breath. My bowels let loose. Snaky tongues lashed at me, violating every orifice on my body.

I lost all track of my senses. My sheer terror flipped like a switch into comatose shock. I turned numb and cold, but the creature kept me warm. It seemed endless. I was hauled through one section to another, each more terrifying than the last. Tiny tentacles examined the labyrinth of my inner ear in a fashion that no Q-Tip was ever meant to. Tongues slithered up my nostrils like filthy nightcrawlers, squirming around, fondling every part of my nasal passages with obscene pleasure. These were the most horrifying moments of my life. I squealed and scratched and begged for it to stop. Angered, it ripped out my fingernails for causing it pain. Finally, the snaily feelers retreated, leaving nasty pus trails inside me.

I was swiftly carried to another section. I could hear a grotesque moaning now, as the thing began to enjoy itself more and more. The flesh here felt like Jell-O and smelled like a combination of putrid Pepto Bismol and turpentine. A huge protuberance was abruptly shoved down my throat. It flexed around through my esophagus down into my stomach, sucking up all the bile, acid, and leftover foods. I could hear slurping noises and groans of pleasure, as if it were tasting my leftovers and enjoying them immensely. In my fear I couldn't fathom what this thing was or why this was happening to me.

The next chamber was the worst of all. These membranes felt like the fatty armpits of obese old humans. The stench was unbearable, as if a constant orgy of nursing home refugees had been going on for eons. More tentacles attacked. This time they went for my junk. A tentacle that was not as thin as I would have wanted entered my urethra and painfully spindled its way into my ball sac. It wandered around, sucking out my sperm. Another tendril penetrated my sphincter, sliding into my bowels. It raced around, scooping up all the compacted waste along my intestines as if it were Nutella.

I heard the creature burping and farting as if it had just wolfed down a gourmet meal. The gases assailed me, forcing me to dry heave the few drops of internal juices I still had left. I was immensely relieved that it seemed to be finished with me. But then I was shuffled back to the first atrium. Those horrible nightcrawlers returned, squishing back up through my septum. They forced their way deeper and deeper, until it felt as if they broke through tissue and reached my brain.

I guess human brains really don't have any pain receptors, because they weren't hurting me. But there was an unbearably creepy sensation of them swirling around inside my skull. Although extremely gentle, their presence caused me to have insane reactions depending on what sections they touched. I laughed hysterically when one swiped past the top right part. When another worm squished across the front of my cerebrum, I became intensely angry. Had a legit reason for that emotion. A third slid over a different segment, my entire body convulsed with uncontrollable fear. My heartrate exploded, my breathing turned to panting, my skin crawled.

But these all appeared and vanished very quickly. They were mainly concerned with the top of my brain near the back of my skull. I would later do research and discover that was the parietal lobe, which interprets signals from other parts of the body. Temperature, pain, touch, sight. And most importantly, taste and smell. They grooved around that portion quite intensely. I got chills, goosebumps popped up on my skin, the hairs on the back of my neck shot up like soldiers coming to attention. Although the creatures contact up there was quite delicate, the thought of them invading my cranial cavity, along with everything else I experienced, finally freaked me out to the point that I blacked out.

Alex and the boys got into some serious trouble when my parents noticed I never came home. They organized a massive search party which scoured the entire county. Cops investigating found plenty of witnesses that said I went to the farm with them the night before. The Temple elders were overly cooperative and let them search anywhere and everywhere. No one could ever find a trace of evidence pointing to their guilt in the matter. The soft spot in the earth where I had fallen in was never found. Officials did find a steamroller with fresh dirt on it, which aroused suspicions. But the monk farmers explained they were flattening out a new road to the orchards.

Time passed, and I became a new chapter in the urban legends of our hometown. My disappearance led the news on every channel for days. I was given up for dead. Funeral arrangements were considered. My buddies were arrested but released to their parents due to lack of evidence. Ex-girlfriends cried, relatives mourned, a candlelight vigil was held. A kind of morbid satisfaction blanketed my fellow citizens. They found comfort in the attention they were receiving from the interviews and the cameras everywhere. Local businesses saw their profits double that week.

I was found nine days later, naked and abandoned in a culvert near a different farm twenty miles away. An old lady on her way to a swap meet after church spotted my butt shining in the morning sun. For reasons doctors couldn't explain, my body showed very few effects of hypothermia, even though the weather was cold enough at daybreak to create a solid frost over everything. I was transported to a hospital, but I couldn't remember anything. Not even my name. Babbled like an idiot, mostly. Deep, monotone words that sounded like gibberish but held an unknown meaning for me.

I was shipped off to Stanford University, where they had one of the finest treatment programs for amnesia patients. Got to go live in California after all. Thanks Mom and Dad. They could have sent me to the Mayo Clinic. Brrrr. It took months, but I slowly recovered most of the memories I had lost. Got so many x-rays and CAT scans, I practically glowed in the dark from radiation. They could never figure out how my brain showed traces of damage inside my skull without any surgery. And the original medical team had found microscopic DNA from some unknown lifeform. Baffled experts were brought in from every continent. They travelled back to the area where I went missing. They never found any hint of a cryptid creature.

Eventually, I tried to rescue what little remained of my former existence. Started taking classes. As my mind grew stronger, I picked out a full schedule. No interest in computers anymore. Took pre-med and battled through until I earned my degree in psychology. Opened an office nearby. Did pretty well for years. Then, one by one, my patients figured out I was crazier than they were. Bizarre dreams I could never remember haunted my conscious life. I would catch glimpses of the blurry monster in broad daylight when no one else saw anything. I had sudden severe twitches, as if some invisible thing stretched out of nowhere to invade my body.

Finally lost my practice. Started a construction company. Went from one van and a sleazy office up to where I had 250 people subcontracting for me. Opened up a "social club" across the street which was only open to "members." I paid my workers in cash, then invited them to my club. There, they proceeded to trade me back all the money I had just paid them for beer and booze I bought wholesale from the local liquor store. It was a gold mine. I was making bank loads of cash. But something was still missing. The part of me that I lost during my disappearance.

I had never returned home in all that time. A dread electrified my spinal column every time I even considered it. But I knew I had to go back. Something waited for me. I believed it was a shred of the lost soul I had left behind. All these years I had felt less than human. Like part of my spirit was still roaming those woods, frightened and lonely. Yes, I was alive. My body functioned. I worked and went shopping, and did all the things that normal people do. But I felt so alienated. As if I was only half a being. I had to go home and rescue my id. Reunite with the person I used to be.

I never told anyone, just hopped on a flight and rented a car at the nearest airport. I was going to surprise my friends and relatives. Have the big party where I catch up on everybody's lives. Laugh about the old times and drink until we pass out. But that was never to be. Because as I drove to my parents' house, I felt this dragging urge in my guts. Someone or something was calling out to me. The closer I drove towards town, the stronger it became.

Then I spotted a farm stand on the side of the road. An electrical storm enveloped my brain. It misfired and short circuited. Felt like lightning struck a power line and it fell to the asphalt during a thunderstorm, sparkling as it bounced around inside my dome. There were the members of the Lunar Ether Temple, selling their wares. They had pitched a tent which stretched block long. A twitch shot down my leg, jolting my foot into hitting the brakes. I inadvertently screeched to a halt, nearly causing a chain reaction auto accident.

I drove off the road into the same culvert where I had been found over a decade before. I jumped out of the vehicle to a nasty chorus of angrily beeping car horns. Ordinarily, I would give them all the finger and probably start brawling with the other drivers. Instead, I cut them off by running directly in their path towards the market. More furious honking assailed my ears, but I tuned it all out. Practically flew across the gravel lot, racing under the canopy to be near the Temple members. Like a moth to a flame, I flew directly into the heart of evil.

Table after table lined up end to end, packed tightly with bushel baskets overflowing with produce. I couldn't even wait in line to buy them, I just started wolfing them down like a starving animal. I poured an entire carton of blueberries down my throat, hardly even chewing. Ignored the shocked faces of the crowd as I stuffed fistfuls of cherries into my overstuffed mouth, swallowing the pits, stems and all. Biting huge chunks of peaches and plums, tossing the remnants to the ground. My face and hands were covered in sticky juices. They were the tastiest foods I had ever eaten. Moans of pleasure filled the air. It was almost orgasmic.

People stared at me as if I was a raving lunatic. And I was. They were like the foods of the gods. I was like Hercules returning to Mount Olympus, feasting on the bounty of the immortals. How could food be so luscious. They all fit my palate like a hand measured Gucci suit. It was almost as if my taste buds had somehow been tested and these foods had been grown…

Oh my god. So that's what the creature was doing. What it had always done. Analyzed the pleasure centers of victim's brains to calculate what tasted good to them. Over the centuries, it captured untold numbers of test subjects. Used the data to modify the plants. Fertilize the soil. Add just the perfect amounts of minerals. Mix in exact measurements of sand, peat, and bark. No wonder their farms were world renowned. A monster data collector lived under their orchards, using lab rats like me to create the perfect products.

The temple members recognized who I was and dragged me away to one of their trucks as I gobbled down whatever else I could grab. They drove me back to their main house while I was in a daze. As they pulled me from the seat, I heard the spirit that had been ripped from my being so long ago calling out to me. Or was it simply the beast, cruelly toying with my emotions? I raced to the spot of my first encounter. I witnessed the earth churning up from below. I dove headfirst into the soil. The monster bubbled over with joy, laughing gleefully and moaning in ecstasy.

I was home now. My destiny had changed forever. I was not going to become some cog in a corporate machine, living a shallow, meaningless life. I had rejoined whatever part of me that was stolen years earlier and mingled with the beast. Writhing in the bowels of this exquisite lifeform, I felt completely fulfilled for perhaps the first time in my insipid time on this planet. And from now on until my end, I will be a part of the Earth itself. The monks have explained their teachings to me. Their beliefs made so much sense. The outside people are destroying this planet, and they will suffer for it. Terra is alive and sentient. It will bring more floods and plagues and wither unholy humanity into extinction. This will be where the new Garden of Eden shall grow for the next generation of inhabitants.

Nano Bites

Things have been going really well lately, which kind of caught me by surprise. Growing up as a Gen Z kid was never easy. My grandmother bought her place back in 1990 for $115,000. A beautiful brick bungalow with three bedrooms, two bathrooms and a garage out back by the alley. It's now worth almost a million. How are we ever supposed to afford that?

With today's inflation, I blow every penny I make on just the bare necessities. People tell us to go to college so we can find something that pays better, but they don't know or care how hard it is to pay for it. I was raised by a single mom with three kids who had to work two different jobs just to put food on the table and clothes on our backs. Maybe if our dad paid child support instead of running off like a bitch and leaving us destitute, she could have put away a few dollars for tuition.

And then mom got COPD. Yeah, she smoked more than the chimney at the local oil refinery, but what do you expect? She was hooked on menthols by the time she got her first period. Her friends got her started. They were all puffing away in the alleys before they even hit high school. She survived on coffee and those evil little sticks of doom which helped her ride the tornado of raising a bunch of crazy kids and working her ass off without any help from her drunk bastard husband.

Then dealing with him leaving and the pervy bosses at work

riding her ass to fill some impossible quotas took its toll. She couldn't stop puffing away, even after the oxygen tanks and the expensive operations left her looking like some zombie from a cheapo horror flick.

Towards the end, I was forced to take care of the medical bills. They were staggering. Every trip to the mailbox made my guts wrench and twist. Whatever little she had stashed away was gone in a few months. Grandma had disowned her years ago for marrying my asshole father and wouldn't lift a finger to help.

My two older siblings ditched us just like the old man. My sister now rides the stripper pole in Florida and my brother panhandles for meth money out in Texas. I was the only one who stuck around to care of her, the way she cared for us growing up. I kept texting them, begging for any little help they could give, but they stopped responding. I guess some people are born with no soul.

After she died, I had to work two jobs to support myself. I didn't have any time to go to trade school. I could barely fit in a few hours a day to sleep. I was too broke to move, and there were no jobs anywhere nearby that paid much more than minimum wage. Even though I was hotter than my sister, lap dancing on fat sweaty losers every night seemed like a fate worse than this pitiful life I already had.

So, after working my butt off since high school, and a little gift loan from my granny, I was finally able to afford to move to a place where decent careers were available. Memphis, The Home of the Blues. Which was kind of fitting, because my whole life seemed to be one melancholy disaster after another.

I found a studio apartment in a semi-livable neighborhood. Literally just a bed, a bathroom, and a kitchenette all in one room.

It was like living in a trailer park, but I was used to that. I got a sales job. Turned out I was pretty good at it. Made "Salesperson of the Year" as a 25-year-old rookie. Things were looking up. I had hope.

Besides having to leave my family and friends behind, one of the hardest things I had to do was change my style. I had been a major goth. Leather and lace. Black fishnet stockings and combat boots. Spiderweb silk gloves and pleated skull miniskirts. Anything and everything dark or evil. Thrift stores were my treasure troves.

Realizing your future is bleak sort of warps your mindset. If I wanted to make a good impression at interviews, that all needed to change. Luckily, I never got any Satanic tattoos. Well, none that my bosses would be able to see. I guess even when I was younger, something in the back of my brain told me conforming to normie society was my only path to staying alive past thirty.

But that didn't mean I didn't still love that way of life. Whenever I had any time and energy left, I cruised the few local clubs that had goth nights. Met people with the same "OK BOOMER!" anger and frustration that I had. But I could never afford those fifteen-dollar martinis. I always thanked the guys who bought me drinks thinking that they were purchasing some magic ticket to my joy ride. But those tough guy wanna-be's who thought buying one cocktail meant they could have their way with me were kicked to the curb. Most of the time.

Not that I'm some celibate whacko. I have needs, too. But the sweetest ones got the luckiest.

I wasn't doing them in a slutty way. I needed a connection. Leaving everybody I loved two hundred miles away hurt my heart. Left my soul as empty as my bank account. Their warmth, their closeness was like an antidote for the sad, lonely nights in the big city.

And what single girl isn't looking for Mr. Right? Someone to build a future with. There has to be a good guy out there who will love me for me. My inner being. Otherwise, what's the point of living? What's the point of anything?

Well, other than online shopping. It's not a cure-all. More like a temporary bandage that stopped my spirit from bleeding out. Tonight, I was going to have a *ménage à trois*. My bed, my phone and me. Few things gave me more pleasure. I've actually kicked guys out after sex so I could swipe and scroll. They had done their part, now it was me-time. Chokers, jewelry, and of course, shoes. Even temporary tats. Tacky, I know, but great on three-day weekends where they wear off by Tuesday.

Last night, I was on a roll, scanning site after site. Not buying much. Just window browsing gave me this regal sense of satisfaction. I played make-believe, acting as if I was filthy rich and could afford to purchase anything I desired. Bookmarking the sweetest items, hoping to buy them sometime in the future. Leaving bad reviews for the ugly crap and making fun of the dumb bitches who bought them. It kept me from feeling isolated.

Even after a year, I didn't have many friends here that I felt comfortable with. I'm a strange creature. An introverted extrovert. I can blab away on a superficial level to just about anybody. But I only feel totally comfortable with a select few. And they were all so far away. The little girl in me still existed as this tiny voice in my heart. She cried constantly. I had to drink or shop or find something that kept her sadness from overwhelming me. I was forced by circumstances beyond my control to run away from home, and I desperately wanted to return. Back to the serenity of my youth. My mom's delicious cooking and my sibling's compassionate antagonisms.

Adulting is hard. It's even harder when your heart aches night after night, because your brain makes you feel like you'll never find your true place in this world. Spending all day surrounded by so many people, like sardines in a subway car. Then going home to unbearable isolation, like that one tiny, twinkling star in an otherwise desolate night sky.

But cybershopping eased my anxiety, dragged me out of the depths of depression. While my swiping fingers were flying and my eyes were glossing over so many gorgeous items I simply had to have, the problems in my head evaporated. It got me high without drugs or drinking or yoga or meditation. My mind went flying on a magic carpet ride inside this incredible hand-held device. There was no way I could be suicidal while I swam through this ocean of commercialism.

Then something really caught my eye. Made my thumb stop dead in its tracks and counter-spin backwards in order to find it again. I thought I knew every single one of these companies. Every night I scoured the same Goth sites over and over. I mean, there are only so many places that make clothes for the eternally somber.

Yet this one was new. Different. So savage. Demonic trinkets that made my buyer's taste buds salivate. Gorgeous earrings I just had to have; with strange symbols I had never seen before. Spiked black leather chokers with ominous demon faces which I just couldn't take my eyes off of.

I knew in the back of my mind that my funds were depleted, but I just had to own these items. Wearing them would make me feel like I was worth something, like my pathetic little life had some meaning to it. My hands trembled as I tapped the buy now icon and sent them to my cart. I had memorized my sixteen-digit debit card number. Against my better judgement, my greedy little fingers pressed complete purchase. It brought a sense of euphoria that fought back the "*You dumbass*" voice echoing from the back of my mind.

But it also brought something else. Something malevolent.

My phone started to feel warm in my hand. As if the battery was overheating. It got so hot, I had to toss it onto the bed. I freaked and jumped off, staring at it, hoping it didn't explode and set the building on fire. The picture on the screen changed from my purchase bill into a weird jumble of bizarre symbols and numerals. It scrambled around, a mini vortex of computer malware hieroglyphs. Lines of code appeared and disappeared at lightning speed. Suddenly, an almost inaudible blip popped in my ears, and I saw something invisible emerge abruptly from the screen.

I realize how seeing something invisible sounds crazy, but it's the only way I could describe what happened. An infinitesimal dot of blur rose up and began to grow. I can only describe it as the pixel disguise they use to hide a nude body part on TV. This wasn't just some eye floater. This was a sentient creature. A ghost from the machine.

But what the hell could it be? A nano-probe from some creepy corporate data thieves? It hovered above the mattress for a long while, and I was too startled to do anything but gaze at it like a mannequin in a store window. Then, in an instant, it shot right at me, centimeters from my face. An imperceivable entity, glaring into my eyes. Then even deeper, into the depths of my soul.

I felt as if I was being probed. It sent out a sensor array which seemed to be scanning my brain, probing my most closely guarded thoughts. All my secrets, things I was too embarrassed to even admit to myself, were laid bare before this entity. My shame-o-meter needle buried itself into the red danger zone. It dragged out every embarrassing kink and fetish, every lewd sex act, every deviant thought that had ever crossed my mind.

Then it concentrated on my effectiveness as a human. What I was good at. What my weaknesses were. A supernatural job interview that felt more humiliating than a cavity search.

Seemingly satisfied, it decided to take a quick cruise around my little hovel. I heard a bizarre screech, and the refrigerator door opened. It saw mustard, a package of low sodium turkey lunchmeat, three pieces of leftover pizza and a half bottle of cheap chardonnay. Each cabinet opened one by one. Each drawer opened, was analyzed, then shut. It dug into every crevice.

In the bottom it found my love bunny vibrator and, even more embarrassing, my handwritten diary. All my hopes, dreams and desires. It immersed itself in the most intimate aspects of my being. My brain told my legs to chase it, for my hands to catch it and smash it into a million shards. But this specter sent out this force which paralyzed me, froze me into a living statue, like the poor buried souls from Pompei who stood helpless as the volcano engulfed them.

Then it zoomed its attention back over at me. This clandestine drone which emerged from inside my Android. It circled my head, around and around. I attempted to get away, but it emitted a strange energy that enveloped my skull. Made me dizzy. Kept me off balance. Hypnotized me.

Then it began to resonate with a kind of music. Electronic, yes, but primordial. Chords and rhythms like I had never heard before. Melodic dirges which engulfed me, enraptured me. Demonic beats which forced my entire body to dance, a tempest of flesh and blood, worshipping this ethereal entity.

The force lifted me right off the ground, as if the laws of gravity never existed. Then my spirit began to pulse, and I gyrated in a frenzy, alone in some satanic mosh pit. I dangled with no control over my movements, and no desire to make it stop. This being was my Master and I was its plaything.

Finally, I understood, and gave myself up. It was then that my new enslaver pleasured me, right there up four feet from the floor. My moans escalated into wails. I experienced an ecstasy I never could have imagined existed, even in my wildest fantasies. Orgasmic seizures hat would have been mistaken for demonic possession by even the most highly trained exorcist.

And then it tossed to the mattress like a pile of dirty clothes on laundry day.

I couldn't still my body, it quivered and quaked in the thralls of euphoria. In the back of my mind, I realized I should have attempted to escape right then and there, but by this time I was its helpless slave. I watched motionless and terror-stricken as it slowly crept through the air towards my eyes, making one final analysis of my worthiness to serve.

Then it slowly whirled around to the right side of my face and entered my ear. It circled around the labyrinth of the canals inside, till it reached my brain. A spark of electricity shocked me from the inside. Made my eyes twitch. I instantly knew that part is known as the temporal lobe, which records auditory information and processes memories.

In fact, there was a bright flare of information which electrified the inside of my skull with a rave of data. Like a flash drive connected directly to my cerebrum. Things that it wanted me to know. Things it wanted me to do. It also began deleting things it didn't want me to possess anymore. Goals. Dreams. Free will. Thoughts of true love and a successful career.

After a few fleeting moments, it had finished with me. I drifted off into the most peaceful sleep I'd had since I was a little girl, and my parents were still together, and everything was right with the world.

When I awoke, my phone was on the pillow next to me, practically staring me in the face. I remember thinking that I should have been afraid of it after the events of the previous night. Instead, there was this profound link between us. I felt as if it were my lover, my master, my reason for being. My hand stretched out in horror, not because I was frightened of it, but because I thought it might have been damaged from the heat.

As my fingertips made contact, it erupted with more jumbles across the screen. Those crazy streams of insane data now made perfect sense to me. They were orders. And I obeyed them instantly, without question.

First, I immediately called my supervisors and quit those disgusting jobs. I had always wished for the courage to tell them all to fuck off and die, but common sense told me it was either work for the man or starve in the streets. Now I had a new lord, and he gave me the confidence to abandon the life I was living. To totally trash my entire existence. Trade it all in for something so much better. A life worshipping the demon in my Android.

I leapt from my bed and showered. This was no ordinary rinse and run, but my baptism into my new life. I scoured every last vestige of my old ways from my skin and my mind, until my flesh was nearly raw, and my brain was nearly blank. I left my old identity swirling in the tub drain behind me. I was now a completely different being, with a new purpose in life.

Got dressed in my hottest, most demonic outfit, then left my room forever. Even though I had no idea where I was going to live or how I was going to exist, I knew as the door slammed behind me that I would never come back again. It was both the most exhilarating and terrifying moment I had ever experienced.

I had no clue where I was heading. My feet took me where I was supposed to go. I had no control, just an automaton guided by the will of my master. I barely noticed where I was heading. Nothing registered except the desire to reach him as fast as mortally possible.

Ended up on a rattling trolley heading to the outskirts of town. It was clean and orderly, yet seemed much older than the ordinary train cars I was used to. Some kind of antique that you only see in museums. Felt weird to be the only passenger. Got out at some bizarre stop I never knew existed. A limo was waiting, sleek, black, and so inviting. I always wanted to know what it felt like to live in luxury. Now I would know forever, as long as I obeyed my dark god.

The driver said nothing, just spun me across a dizzying series of back roads so quickly that I couldn't have memorized the directions if I wanted to. The colors and lifeforce of the city paled as we headed on our way. The further we went along the route, the more barren and lifeless the forest grew. The bright, happy sunshine gloomed away into bleakness until it almost seemed to be night. The entire journey was apocalyptic.

I didn't sense time as I used to before. None of the worry of waking up to the alarm early enough to get to work. No rage at traffic when it was making me late. There was no feeling of boredom when things seemed to be taking forever. No thrill when there was nothing but clear roads ahead. Only a strict urgency to get to where my master wanted me to be.

All I could think of now was that entity I interfaced with through my phone the night before. I now knew who and what he was. The Ancient One, summoned from his primeval slumber. Pitiful mortals who thought they were the true owners of this planet had turned it from sweetness and light unto the bitter darkness of hatred, violence, and blasphemy. The vast majority of men and women of our world had now become more evil than good.

It was time for The Cleansing. Not the slaughter of the wicked, but the genocide of the holier than thou.

Soon we arrived in front of an old gothic church, as desolate as any building I had ever seen. I walked up to the huge black wooden doors, which squeaked open by themselves. The interior was just as empty as the roads I had travelled to get here. Dozens of rows of empty pews, enough to fit hundreds of people. Wrought iron torches hung along the walls, illuminating sculptures of martyrs being tortured. But these were not sinners, they were saints. The worshippers of love and decency, whipped into a frenzy for failing to idolize our true master.

Arrassakka. The one from before time. He who twisted men's dreams. Stripped them of their humanity. Forced them to realize war and brutality were their genuine philosophies. He who was my new god.

I found a secret door behind the altar as if I always knew it was there. Inside was a spiral staircase which seemed to go on forever, deep into the very bowels of the earth. Finally, I arrived at the Great Hall for my indoctrination. A monstrously huge cavern, covered with stalactites and stalagmites. Thousands of fellow disciples had already arrived. I joined in and immersed myself with their faith. We all chanted his name again and again:

Arrassakka, Arrassakka, Arrassakka.

And then Arrassakka appeared to us, floating through the very crust of the earth from his own private corner of Hell. A sight so unbearably terrifying that many had their eyes sizzle away in their sockets. The unworthy had their tongues ripped from their mouths by invisible forces before they could utter his name once more. The god of all gods, whose visage drove the weakest of us to a madness so painful, they screamed and writhed in unbearable agony until they perished in an explosion of gore. Only the strongest and most devoted of us survived.

We stripped off all our clothing and writhed around with each other in a gigantic orgy in the Divine One's honor. I shall have many babies and teach them all that Arrassakka is our true Master. We will join together with other groups on every continent and create the largest army the world has ever seen. We will conquer the disbelievers and slaughter all who refuse to conform. Their death echoes will feed our lord with the energy he needs to rule once more. He will return to the skies above the earth and wreak havoc with the ways of men.

I am much happier now. I no longer have the fears and the sorrows that have plagued me since childhood. My true lord is all that I shall ever desire. Arrassakka's will is my command. Tonight, I go back to the clubs. I will find a suitable mate and bring him home. For sex, then for sacrifice. He shall know the glory of dying for the Only One. His soul will be energy for my master. Food to keep him strong while we carry out his orders.

We shall slaughter all the infidels who glorify the false gods of humankind. Kindness and charity are blasphemies. Murder and hatred are our true calling. Death for all who fail to devote their existence to Arrassakka.

By the way, what are you shopping for tonight?

Melvin and Me

Life has been sucking bad lately. Jobs suck too. That's because I have two of them. They both blow chunks. Bosses blow. Coworkers, too. Can't stand what they make me do. Can't stand any of it. I work so hard, but they hardly give me no money.

Life was better when I was a kid. Mom had money. She had a nice house where we lived. We had breakfast and TV. But then policemen came and took her away. Then other men in nice suits put her in a big box. They dug a big hole in the ground and put her in there. I wanted to go live with her down there but people stopped me.

She stayed down there and left me all alone. Fancy people took our house away. Told me to go get a job and not be a burden on society. Now I live in my car. Wash up at the beach.

One day at work I was scrubbing toilets. The floor was slippery. I slipped and hit my head real hard. My eyes saw a zillion stars. Like when my grandpa took me fishing in the country. When I opened my eyes, I saw my brain fell out of my head. It bounced behind the garbage can.

I was bleeding but felt a lot better. I walked out to the office and told my bosses to fuck off. They looked at me scared but said okay, I could go. Went to the beach.

The beach felt nicer that day without my brain. I didn't care that stupid people threw their garbage all over. I didn't care that rich people threw all their chemicals into the water, so it was too dirty to go swimming. I didn't care that bad cops beat up that black kid just for talking to white girls.

This was much better. Life didn't hurt. Everything was pretty to me. Made me happy.

Two kids asked if they could bury me in the sand. I said sure. They dug a hole real deep. But they forgot to leave a place for me to breathe. Silly kids. I couldn't breathe not hardly at all. Lots of sand in my mouth. I got tired. Went to sleep. Slept for a long time.

Woke up and felt better. Dug my way out. Everybody went home and left me there. But I didn't cry. I figured maybe I would still need my brain sometime. Walked back to work. It was still there, but a big rat was gnawing on it. I had to fight for it, because the rat wouldn't let go. I thought it would scare me, but I didn't care.

How did it fall out? I didn't know. Mom told me life is full of mystery and what fun would it be if I knew everything? I shoved my brain back into my head. It went right in, but the rat went with it. Ran around in there like crazy. Trapped like in a cage. It bit and scratched but couldn't get out.

I went ow ow ow and shook it around, but the rat was stuck. I scratched at my brain, but it stayed locked up inside. But then it stopped caring. Just like me. It started being happy in there. It liked my little cage. I liked him being in there, too. I named him Melvin.

We went back to the beach. I quit my jobs because they sucked. I live behind the garbage now. I met all of Melvin's friends. We share each other's food and play rat games all night when the people go away. When someone is mean to me, Melvin tells me what to do. When they walk away, I hit them hard. His buddies eat them up after. Lately when I'm hungry, I eat them, too. Then I bury them like the kids buried me. The beach has a lot of deep holes.

Now Melvin had babies inside my head. I guess she is Melvina. They run around like crazy. It tickles and we all laugh and laugh. Everyone needs a Melvin. You want to adopt one of her babies?

Lake of the Lost

When I first spotted the invitation, I was more than just suspicious. I was a little pissed off. I lived in a gated community with extra heavy security. LA is a tough town, even for a battle-tested Hollywood stuntman like me. Nobody was supposed to be able to get in or out without a resident's authorization. I had bounced out of bed at dawn for a ten-mile run, and when I got back, there it was. Sitting on my kitchen table. An odd-shaped envelope with my name etched across the front, leaning up against the smoothie blender cup I had just emptied ninety minutes earlier.

Someone had broken into my home.

My lips curled up involuntarily, my fists squeezed tight. This was bullshit. Three things in life I refused to put up with; "yo mama" jokes, messing with my ride, or messing with my crib. I grabbed my Glock 17 from its permanent spot on top of the fridge, then prowled each and every room in the house. Nobody. I checked all the doors and windows in each room, but they were still securely locked from the inside. Nothing of any value had been stolen.

My place was airtight. I made sure of that before I moved in six years earlier. No resident had reported any burglaries or vandalism or even an unwanted visitor in all that time. I phoned the front gate personnel, and they said that nobody had been buzzed in or out since midnight. How did it simply appear in my condo? Sorcery?

I noticed the packet was made of thick, heavy stock, not the thin junk mail paper everything else shows up in. It almost seemed to be goatskin parchment. Real stuff, not the new simulated kind. Around four by six inches, without my address or a return address. And it was actually sealed on the back with red wax, bearing several strange symbols I had never seen before. This was the way kings and knights of the Middle Ages kept their official correspondence secret from the prying eyes of the couriers. Intriguing.

I had become recognized as an authority on ancient cyphers and hieroglyphs for over a decade. Ever since I started getting hired as a stunt man on some of the biggest fantasy blockbusters. The Hobbit. Game of Thrones. Always playing the double of the biggest, toughest warriors. Spent years training with the best, learning hand to hand combat and the art of battle with medieval weapons. Broadswords, axes, maces. Now I was the man who all the studio hotshots called first when a new fantasy project gets greenlit.

The languages of the many mythological races in these books caught my attention. I became fascinated with the different icons and alphabets. Calligraphy is truly an art form. Yet I had never seen anything like the markings embossed onto this sachet. I grabbed some scissors and carefully cut a slice through the top, so I could remove the contents without damaging the seal.

After turning it sideways, a single airplane ticket slipped out. I snatched it midair before it fell to the ground. It had an open departure time from LAX to the Idaho Falls Regional Airport. Not exactly a hot tourist destination. The invite was also made of the same material, written in an Old English font which evolved in the twelfth century. It said simply…

"Duncan Rainier, you are hereby expected to report to our

awaiting aircraft immediately. Arrangements have been made to transport you to accommodations at Lake Portae in Wyoming."

Not exactly a tantalizing request. I googled Lake Portae and found no links to it. Went to my Mac and checked the entire state map with magnified views and found absolutely no trace of it. Either this was an elaborate practical joke, or something very strange was going on. I couldn't think of anyone who would want to screw with me.

Yes, my late teens and early twenties were a little crazy. I'm not ashamed to admit I left a trail of angry fathers across the small town I grew up in and a gang of suspicious police officers at the campus where I went to college. But that had all ended many years ago. Since then, I had become a loner, preferring comfortable silence to loud parties and people calling at all hours. Friendly, but not engaging.

My business dealings had always been honest. My phone contained a contact list filled with ladies who were more than happy to stop by for one-night stands when I got the urge. Always avoided anyone married or with serious entanglements. Couldn't think of anyone in recent memory pissed off at me enough to pull a stunt like this.

And those few who I do occasionally socialize with know that messing with me is not a smart idea. I was an MMA fighter, although my career was short lived. I was undefeated in eight bouts but didn't enjoy it. Beating the shit out of other human beings was not my concept of a satisfying career path. Found it repulsive. The money was great, but I didn't have that sadistic urge inside me.

I had spent my school years protecting other kids from bullies. If my opponents were inside the cage stomping on the less fortunate, I would have been more than happy to charge in and whoop their asses. But pounding a worthy combatant into the canvas for kicks made me cringe. Turned down boatloads of cash. Promoters thought I was gonzo. I returned to TV and movie work on the best of terms with the guys I fought. Had the feeling they were happy to get rid of me.

So, what the hell was with this letter? I tossed it on the counter and noticed something weird. It began to dissolve. I tried to snatch it back up, but it melted in my hand like candle wax. This was becoming more and more mysterious. Life today had become so computerized and digitized. Electronic gadgetry bored me. I always had a soft spot for the mythic, magical ages of history. And a solo trip to the great outdoors sounded great. No sixteen-hour days working with cocky actors and overstressed film crews. This was perfect timing because I…

…I had two months of work on a martial arts flick mysteriously cancelled… just last night. It was set to start in three days, but the producers suddenly had cash flow problems. So, I had no obligations for the foreseeable future. What the hell was going on? Were the people who delivered this cryptic message responsible for terminating the project?

I instinctively slammed my hand on the table, sending the smoothie cup spinning in a circle, beet-red droplets bleeding across the wooden surface. The curiosity I had felt flicked like a switch to seething resentment. I tried calling the movie execs, but none of them offered any explanations, just that I would be compensated for any lost revenue. So, I phoned the airport to confirm my flight. They said the pilot was on standby 24/7. Refused to answer any other questions.

Someone had ensnared me into this bullshit game, and I didn't like being played. But the only way I would find the answers was to become a pawn. Join in and fly to Idaho. I packed my suitcase and went to get cleaned up.

Why do people do most of their best thinking in the shower? Just a few moments into rinsing the sweat from my body, a light bulb flashed on. I realized I was probably being “Punk’d.” One or more of my old party buddies had gotten together to drag me out of the house for a weekend of revelry. They’ve all been bugging me for years to come rave it up with them like the good old days ever since I decided to stop partying and concentrate on my career. They were probably waiting for me at the airport with tickets to Vegas.

Our exploits there were legendary. Made the guys from “The Hangover” look like wussies. I began mentally checking down a list of the usual suspects. Before I could even pull my pants on, there was a knock at my door. Wrapped myself in a towel and answered. I thought it would be security checking on my earlier call. But it was a chauffeur, dressed as elegantly as if he were picking up a billionaire. Waiting behind him was a pristine black limousine almost as long as the front of my condo, the motor still running.

“Sir, please come with me. No need for any luggage. All your clothing and other necessities will be provided for you at no cost. I’ll be waiting in the car.”

“Who are you working for? What is all this?” I asked.

“I have none of that information. If you don’t wish to proceed, my employers will be forced to make other arrangements. But I’ve been told that you are by far their most preeminent candidate.”

It was an obvious sales pitch. He was playing to my ego. But it worked. I was hooked. Who had orchestrated this whole spontaneous adventure? What were these qualities of mine that so impressed them? I had plenty of doubts, but this guy seemed straight up legit. I was a good judge of character and could tell by the look in his eyes he was an upstanding citizen just doing his job. And this mystery would haunt me forever if I didn't follow the clues and see it through.

I pulled on some loose fitting jeans and a sweatshirt, strapped on my gun and holster, then covered up with a light jacket. Checked for keys, wallet, and phone, and locked the door behind me. He clicked his FOB and my door glided open. I entered and it slammed and locked behind me. I had no clue whether this would end up being a once in a lifetime joyride or end up painful and bloody. But I was now trapped in this puzzle to the bitter end.

Inside was about as luxurious as you could get. The liquor cabinet contained one bottle of my favorite bourbon and one of the champagne I always drank on New Year's Eve. I opted for the bubbly shit because I was still wary of this whole expedition. I didn't want to get too bombed in case this ended up turning into some gory torture trap.

When we arrived at the airport, I got an even bigger shock. Drove through a private gate, avoiding all security. The plane awaiting me was a Gulfstream G550, one of the most expensive private jets around. Built for sheiks and CEO's. There were no corporate logos, just those same strange symbols from the envelope plastered across the tail assemblage.

The car door unlocked and opened by itself. The driver either couldn't hear or refused to respond to my thank you. Walked up the steps to the entry door and found a single flight attendant smiling as I boarded. Gorgeous girl. Just my type. A true blond with no dark roots or eyebrows. Just tanned enough to look healthy, not leathery. Teeth perfectly straight and gleaming white as the A1 on dental charts.

“Greetings, Mr. Rainier,” she said, completely unfazed by the firearm bulging through my coat. One of those unique symbols was embroidered on her lapel. She gazed at me knowingly, as if we had been friends for years, yet her eyes gave me the once over like she was a party girl looking for a hook-up at a nightclub. “If there is anything you require, please don’t hesitate to let me know.”

“What’s my seat number? It wasn’t on the ticket.”

“Feel free to recline wherever you’d prefer.” she answered, waving me inside.

Turned down the aisle and found I was the only passenger. There was only one leather chair in the entire cabin. A large buffet of different foods and drinks that smelled incredible. And a king-sized bed in the rear which could have come from the honeymoon suite at a five-star hotel, encircled by mirrors which rose to the ceiling. This was no prank. I knew some very wealthy celebrities, but none well enough to blow this kind of cash just to point and laugh at me later.

The moment I sat down and buckled up; the plane started towards the runway. Probably the smoothest takeoff in history. Not a hint of turbulence. The dreaded pressure that always gave me pain deep in my eardrums was nonexistent. If I wasn’t staring out the window, I would have thought I was in an elevator in a fancy hotel headed to the penthouse.

I closed my eyes and felt no motion whatsoever. Almost weightless. As if the seatbelt was the only thing holding me down. Practically in a dream-like state. Perhaps scientists were right. Reality doesn't exist until it is observed. Felt quite content at that moment.

“Hello, Mr. Rainier.” the pilot said over the intercom. “Weather is clear. Our flight will take less than two hours. If you see anything you like, please feel free to indulge yourself."

I turned to the buffet and received another mild shocker. It was filled with small portions of all my favorite dishes. Not the standard filet mignon, lobster, and caviar that the wealthy always seem to prefer. Tikka Masala from India. Dim Sum from China. A chili cheese dog from Pink's on La Brea. It was a smorgasbord of every food that was special to me. As if they knew my exact tastes.

This was getting too weird. My senses were tingling, as if I was in some type of danger. But the aromas were stronger. I surrendered to this gastropub in the sky. Flying 40,000 feet in the air, I was pretty much their prisoner till we landed. My Glock and I would deal with any threats as they confronted me. I selected a few samples and wolfed them down. Exquisite.

The first threat arrived far more quickly than I anticipated. The stewardess sauntered over from the back of the cabin wearing nothing but red lingerie. Push up bra, garter belts, long silk stockings. Breathtaking. As if they sampled my brain waves and built a woman exactly to my erotic specifications. She laid tummy down on the bed, waiting for me like a gift under the Christmas tree waiting to be unwrapped.

"I hope you haven't overstuffed yourself. We have plenty of time before we land," she said.

Hell with it, figured I was already waist-deep in this escapade, might as well enjoy the entire experience. I had already been a card-carrying member of the Mile High Club, but sex in a tiny jet bathroom is not as pleasurable as it might seem. The knocking on the door from antsy passengers keeps interrupting the pounding going on inside.

This was a whole different animal. Out in the open, with all the room you could ever desire. None of the begging for you to finish quick. This babe was wilder than any fantasy girl I could dream up. Must have been a gold medalist in the World Kegel Championships, because she squeezed on tight and refused to let go. Had to fight my way to the finish line. More than happy to come in second place. Several times.

But as we felt the plane descend, and as the tires hit the asphalt, her demeanor changed. She was all back to business as usual. Ran back to the rear compartment without a word. I got dressed and combed back my hair with my hand. We pulled up the tarmac and connected to the boarding bridge. She reappeared fully dressed and opened the hatchway exit. I was about to give her a goodbye kiss, but she gave me the oddest expression.

"Goodbye, Mr. Rainier. Hope you have a successful mission."

"I never got your name."

"It's Eve."

"Well, you were certainly worth any one of my ribs."

She smiled and winked. I was about to ask whether I could see her again, but she quickly slammed the door shut behind me. Had to laugh, because I was always the one slamming the doors behind the females as I escorted them out. Strolled down the hooded corridor until I emerged inside a private gateway. Completely void of life except for another chauffeur. I was shocked to see he was a carbon copy of the one who picked me up in LA. They could have been twins, only this one had red hair instead of blond.

"What the hell. Do you have a brother in California?" I asked, but he was in no mood for small talk.

"Good day, Mr. Rainier. Please follow me."

He led me down to a tunnel where another luxurious limo awaited, this one pure white. Since I was all in at this point, I couldn't resist trying the bourbon. Possibly the finest I'd ever tasted. Had a woodsy spice to it. Definitely aged quite a few years, for it went down smoothly, without that face-twisting burn from the alcohol.

My road trip took about as long as the plane flight. The scenery was more breathtaking than expected. I could tell we were traveling northeast, close to Yellowstone National Park. Ancient land of geysers, hot springs, and extraordinary wildlife. There was a grand canyon here almost as incredible as the more famous one in Arizona. And that super-volcano that scientists say is overdue to explode and destroy all life on earth as we know it.

Perhaps Lake Portae is one of those private areas that the 1% have kept hidden for themselves so none of the common rabble can set foot there. Or maybe it's a top-secret government facility like Area 51 once was, where classified experiments are conducted, and stranded alien lifeforms are kept prisoner. Or possibly this bourbon was spiked with some spacy drug and causing my imagination to overreact.

We came to an unmarked gate that opened automatically for our limo, then pulled onto a long gravel road that went on for miles. One last curve, and the most picturesque log cabin I had ever seen came into view, more beautiful than any Thomas Kinkade painting. Nestled into a natural curve at a mountain's edge, it somehow appeared as old as the hills, yet brand new at the same time.

Behind it lay a pristine lake, more serene than anything Bob Ross could ever create. It truly was a most stunning sight to behold. I barely remember exiting the vehicle and approaching the scene. It was as if I were mesmerized. I had always been more impressed by a well-built rustic cottage than any stately mansion or royal palace. This was my dream home.

I wandered up, inspecting the master craftmanship. Walls made of pine timber stacked horizontally, with a high-pitched gable roof for the snow to slide off, and purlin logs attached to a ridge beam at the peak. A huge deck with overhanging eaves and soffit leading to a long dock straight out into the lake.

I stepped across all the way down the plank floorboards without a single creak. The air I breathed in invigorated me, like the oxygenated atmosphere inside a casino. The water was so crystal clear I could see the bottom as far as my eyes could perceive. Two fishing poles hung in an outdoor cabinet containing everything an angler could ask for. The finest lures and tackle, even a built-in aquarium filled with live minnows. And a glass door fridge filled with all my favorite beers. This was a genuine paradise.

I turned to ask the chauffeur about something. I don't even recall what it was. But he and the limo had disappeared. Vanished without a sound. Not even the tires crunching the rocks which covered the only route away from here. Could I have been so entranced by this lodge that I didn't hear it? Something wasn't right. But for whatever reason, I didn't care. They had dropped me off at the most beautiful private spot in the world. I was going to enjoy it.

The door to get inside was built as strong as a gate for a medieval castle. In fact, the entire building was solid as a fortress. I walked inside and was pleasantly surprised. Larger than it appeared from the outside. Very Spartan accommodations. Almost military looking, with two long rows of bunk beds along the back walls. A huge kitchen that had restaurant-sized stoves and grill tops. Industrial refrigerator/freezers.

Inside was enough food to feed a small army. Counters with space to prepare meals for large groups of people. A hefty wooden table and a dozen chairs. Two separate bathrooms that had a huge showering area connecting them. And more of those symbols, embossed on silk and engraved in metal, then framed and hung at various intervals throughout the residence.

But no people. I was beginning to wonder if someone thought I had been working too hard and needed a vacation. I did have three long, grueling movie shoots in a row, but I always recovered quickly. I was back to my fighting form, ready for action. There were no landline phones, and my cell picked up zero bars. How was I supposed to call for a lift home?

Still, I wasn't going to let a good thing go to waste. As long as I was stuck here, might as well enjoy it. Fishing and beer in the most picturesque spot I had seen since I worked in New Zealand. Tomorrow I would worry about getting back to LAX. Tonight, I was going to have a blast.

As I walked back outside, I noticed the door had a massive metal barricade. Not the kind you use to keep out burglars. An iron crosspiece beam that slid down into old metal brackets. The kind kings had built to keep bands of crazed marauders from invading their castles.

And every window had hefty, prison-like security bars. Why would anyone install such old-fashioned gadgets in this day and age? Hungry bears? Not likely. This place was built to withstand an all-out war. Vikings attacking a lord's manor type of stuff. Who built this place, and why was it so well-fortified?

Well, this was going to require a lot of deep thought, and there was no better way to sort out life's mysteries than a long night of fishing. I headed back out to the dock and cast out both poles. One with a Rapala floater and the other with a shiner minnow. Double my chances, double my fun. Catch two fish instead of one.

Grabbed a beer out of the fridge. A Moretti's. Love the guy on the label wearing the hat. They had more of that bourbon as well. I leaned back into one of the comfiest outdoors chairs I have ever sat in and sank into my own little world. Nabbed a few keepers. Brown trout, walleye, but not at that one-after-another pace which becomes more exhausting than exciting. Just a steady flow. Catch and release, of course.

The sky got darker, and I saw more stars than I had ever thought possible. It was as if I was staring through the lens of the James Webb telescope. I began to almost visualize the spinning galaxies. Experience the time warp between myself and those galaxies that were staring back at me from billions of years in the past.

I started to space out a bit, feeling at one with the Universe. As if someone was out there, in that unexplainably vast distance, gazing back at me. Communicating with me by telepathy or some paranormal wormhole of the mind. Saying thanks. Wishing me well. Honoring my commitment to the protection of my planet. I couldn't understand what was happening. How they were communicating with me. Whether this was actually happening or a wild hallucination.

Things got hazy and I passed out. The deepest, happiest sleep of my life.

Woke up to the chirping of birds. Still in a daze, but then felt the chill of dawn. Moist dew covering everything. I shuddered and rubbed my eyes, because what I saw stunned me to my feet. The entire lake was gone. Vanished. I saw a cavernous ravine out in the distance where all the remaining water was flowing into. As if it were being channeled into some vast gorge.

The bottom was all rocky and already beginning to dry out in the sun. I jogged around the pier to the shoreline. All the marine life had followed the water. There were no fish flopping around, no crawfish scooting under cover of flat stones. I took a step out and found the craggy bed was easy to navigate. Not slippery from moss or algae. Perhaps I should have run off then and there. But my curiosity was racing even more quickly than my pulse. I couldn't prevent myself from investigating.

The entire landscape had this alien quality to it. Felt as if I were walking across the surface of some distant planet. Gone where no man had gone before. Had to navigate a narrow slope into a far deeper drop-off section, which was steep but manageable. Quick steps took me dozens, then hundreds of feet below the land I had left behind. The terrain then flattened out, but my exhilaration was sky high. It was like exploring a mysterious lost cave without all the claustrophobia.

I began to discover fossils on the ground. Primeval species of aquatic creatures which existed millennia ago. Then artifacts. The Native American arrow heads were easily explainable. But then I found ancient swords and daggers. Even a mace. What were all these strange European weapons doing on the bottom of a lake in Wyoming? And even though they had been underwater for centuries, they bore no rust, nor signs of age. As pristine as the waters of this enigmatic body of water.

Then I felt something. Strange vibrations coming from the ground. An intermittent pounding, so barely perceptible, I had to stop and concentrate just to sense them. I bent to my knees and put my hand to the earth. Sporadic yet prodigious impacts, followed by reverberations, from deep inside the lakebed. Almost like earthquakes, yet not quite the same. What the hell was going on?

Searching ahead, I spotted something large and metallic. A silverish glint sparkling in the midst of the shale and limestone topography. What the hell could that be?

I took off running. The further I got, the more it seemed to grow. I could now tell it was huge. My fascination piqued, I started racing as fast as possible across the ankle-twisting rock bed. It looked circular, nothing that occurred naturally. Yes, definitely round and dozens of feet across.

Random notions flooded my mind. This might be a crashed UFO. Was I going to be the first person on Earth to prove that extraterrestrials exist? My heart raced faster than my feet could take me. A joyous expression appropriated my normally implacable face. As I got closer, I felt a force emanating from the object. An otherworldly sensation.

When I reached it, I saw the same strange symbols embossed onto the metal. Was I being intentionally invited to meet these beings? Were the chauffeurs and stewardess a part of a Men in Black organization? But then it became clear. It wasn't a spaceship. It was some type of hatchway. There were large hinges on one side. It was a gateway to something underground. All that water and marine life had flowed away to reveal this shiny entranceway to some unknown place. My destiny.

But how to open it? And should it even be opened? It could be radioactive inside. Or I might release some deadly virus or bacteria into the atmosphere. I would be responsible for a plague that wiped out humanity. I briefly thought of contacting the government. They have scientists and military professionals who have proper procedures for cases like this.

I couldn't resist at least touching it. What harm could that cause? Was it as hard as diamonds, or soft as a baby's bottom? I reached out tentatively, with just the tip of my index finger.

Instantly, a surge of pure energy electrified my entire body. As if I had been bombarded with a super powerful MRI machine. A weird aquamarine glow surrounded me. I was reenergized, like The Incredible Hulk hit with gamma rays. The hatch opened wide, and my own jaw followed suit. It lifted up into the air without a sound.

Inside was a cavernous tunnel. Not the futuristic technological miracle I was hoping for. But enthralling, nonetheless. There were no lights inside, but somehow my vision could scan deep within, far past the range of sunshine. All my cautions had been thrown to the wind long ago, so I climbed in to investigate. It was a spelunker's dream. The walls seemed to emit a kind of pale illumination, bright enough to guide my way.

There was a well-worn trail leading forward. Dozens, perhaps hundreds of footsteps were fossilized into the stone. Everything from bare human feet to primitive sandals to combat boot prints. That was both a thrill and a disappointment. Obviously, I was not the first person to discover this place. But I still had to uncover the reason I had been brought here.

As I marched further, I began to find more of the weapons. Battle axes, spears, war hammers. All lying on the ground. Then I noticed what appeared to be graffiti on the walls. What the hell? So, this was just an elaborate prank? There, in plain sight, "Killroy was here" was inscribed in a white chalky substance, accompanied by the obligatory cartoon sketch of a bald man with a huge nose hanging over a wall. This was a hugely popular meme during World War II, long before the word meme was invented. What was it doing here?

As I progressed, more words were scribbled on the rock. “Vive la revolution,” the famous slogan of the French back in the 1790’s, when they beheaded King Louis XVI and Marie Antoinette and took back their country. “Gloria Exercitus,” or “To the glory of the army,” the motto of the Roman legions. Others were simply names written in various ancient languages. Sanskrit from India. Hanzi from China. Egyptian and Mayan hieroglyphs. Even cuneiform from Sumeria.

I was really happy that I could sort of understand most of this, because I had studied archaic symbols and vocabularies. Yet there was no explanation for how all these people had been inside this cavern before. There were even cave paintings of bison and deer. Probably Native American, but who knows? They could just as possibly been the work of Cro Magnons.

I could have stayed there and studied these archeological mysteries for weeks, but something kept me trudging forward. That pounding was getting stronger. And now I could hear it. Sounded like enormous thuds smashing against a metallic wall. The further I walked, the louder they got.

I turned a corner into a massive hall, and to my amazement, a series of human-sized sculptures lined the entire area. Hundreds of them. Thousands. Like the Terracotta Army discovered in the 1970s in China. Only these were soldiers of every major civilization on Earth, every era. Males and females. Ninjas. Cherokees. Aborigines. Amazons. Neanderthals. Even bluish, marine-like humanoids, with gills along the neck.

Were these Atlanteans? Amphibious ancestors to Homo Sapiens? All of them were perfectly designed as some kind of memorial tribute. A museum to the proudest champions of Earth’s history. But why were they here?

Nearby was an immense chamber lined with countless rectangular mounds. Tombstones perched upon each one. I trekked across the rows, trying to decipher what they said. Languages from every corner of the planet carved upon them. Dates of birth and death, some fairly recent, others predating all the histories known to modern science. This was a cemetery, hallowed grounds. Who were these people, from such faraway lands and different eras? And why were they buried here, thousands of miles from their homelands?

The pounding became deafening. I had to push forward to see what was causing it. As I delved even deeper into the abyss, I saw it. Another hatchway, exactly like the entranceway behind me. But this one had dents and pockmarks coming from the other side. Something, or things, were hammering on it so hard, it was beginning to bend and crack. It thrummed with every impact. Unknown entities, enormous and powerful, were on the other side, pounding desperately to get through. Whatever they were, there was no way they were friendly.

But how could I stop them by myself? This time, I knew I was in over my head. Me and my Glock were no match for whatever forces were imprisoned behind that doorway. Every time the force struck; it seemed as if this would be the second they crashed through.

I was ready to run back and contact the government. They'd most likely screw everything up, but at least they had the firepower to stop whatever was trying to smash its way up here. Just then, there was a crack in the metal. Just a tiny fracture in the alloy. But it was enough to let a piercing cry infiltrate and echo forth, one that haunted my very soul. A sound like nothing I had ever heard before. The cry of victory from the pits of Hell.

The slit expanded, contorted. An eerie smog gusted in, like

smoke back-drafting out of a burning factory door. It seemed live wired, as if galvanized with an otherworldly electrical current. Sparks stung at my skin.

The smell of rotting flesh mixed with the burning sensation of sulfuric acid singed my nostrils. I tried breathing with my mouth, but the inside skin sizzled from the very air. The pounding continued, tearing a hole into the metal.

I saw a gigantic, hideous orb peering in at me from the other side. Then, a tongue-like appendage shot out at me at warp speed. I barely dove out of its way and rolled aside. It wasted no time squirming after me, sweeping its purplish extremity across the floor of the cave in an attempt to capture me.

I whipped out my handgun and pointed it dead on target, but before I could fire, it melted away into hot jelly and dripped through my fingers. How was this even possible? Obviously, modern weapons were not going to cut it down here. Supernatural forces ruled this cave.

I reached down and found a hatchet lying nearby. Swung it every time the tentacle snapped at me. I backhanded full force and sliced it in half. The creature screamed and dragged its bleeding organ back to the other side.

But this first strike against the enemy also unleashed some type of power. The circular framework around the door began to glow. An electrified beam of light shot out across the entire cavern. It fired through me, but also flashed like lightning bolts at all the individual statues behind me. Sparkling streams of vitality fired into their forms, electrifying them with life-giving energy.

Just as the crack gave way and bent apart, all the countless warriors who I thought were just effigies instantly sparked to life. They all howled out in their own languages, ecstatic to be brought back from dreamland. Warriors reanimated for one more battle. The crusade was on.

Another beast smashed its way through. Gleaming platinum scales covered its throbbing globular shape, a tripod of monstrous claws and gnashing teeth, maybe thirty feet tall and larger in diameter. It called out in some demonic dialect, a combat cry to its comrades shuffling behind.

I fired my hatchet, and it spun around on a direct course, striking the thing in the middle of its head. A gash opened up, and foul blood spurted forth. But it would take a lot more to croak this gigantic bastard.

The others stormed right past me, attacking the shiny creature with swords, spears, and war hammers. Other beasts burst through the fissure. A massive octopus-like being with twenty legs which shot out individually, stinging my new comrades with spiny talons. Three went down immediately before others fired arrows at its head, sending it squealing into oblivion.

Fresh demons emerged out of the gate, each more hideous than the one before. I fell back, shoulder to shoulder with my new mates.

"What the hell is going on?" I yelled.

"Hell, indeed, my fine young friend," an armored knight answered.

"We are The Terra Sentinels," a Viking continued.

"We are chosen by the lords of chaos to protect our world from the devils of the far dimensions," an African female warrior added.

"What am I doing here?" I asked.

“No time for words, my new friend, only life or death,” the Knight said as he charged in.

The others followed, so I raced in alongside. Our one stroke of luck was that the hole was still small, so only a few of these things could squeeze over to our world at a time. But as every monster squeezed into our realm, the crack opened wider. Soon, more and more of them were entering, faster than we could slay them.

They cried out in various foul dialects, resounding with a palpable wickedness to the point that hearing them caused pain. Their words stung my ears with their malevolence. Their decibels drifted up the cave, spreading demonic chants up into our earthly atmosphere.

Was this tunnel the source of all evil on Earth? Where every thought of war, hatred, rape, greed, or murder emanated from? Desecration of anything that is good was escaping from this hellhole towards our people above. It was our job to stop it.

I spotted a fine broadsword which clinked on the rocky floor. As I lifted it from the ground I couldn’t stop an ear-to-ear grin from forming on my face. This was the fantasy I’d been having since I was a kid reading old Conan the Barbarian comic books. Doing battle like the ancients against the foulest of adversaries.

Shoulder to shoulder with my new comrades, we crashed into the frontlines of these supernatural beasts. I had always thought I knew what it would feel like from movies and video games, but nothing could have prepared me for fighting in close quarters at the center of a mythical conflict.

It was as if I had been launched into a hurricane of flashing blades and falling limbs. Everywhere I turned, gore from some just-injured lifeform splattered me in the face. I constantly had to duck from razor-sharp claws or leap away from gaping maws lined with yellowed fangs. There was barely room for me to swing my sword, but when it did, I struck the foul flesh of some otherworldly beast.

This was an insane whirlwind of action I could barely comprehend. The cave blared with the victory cries of those who had slain their adversaries combined with the death howls of those same vanquished protagonists, creating an uproar so deafening I could hardly concentrate on what was happening. My lungs burned from the exertion and excitement, my mind swirled in fear and confusion.

If it weren't for the valiant efforts of my comrades, I would have certainly succumbed to these satanic forces. Watching their brave exploits as they battled back our enemies reenergized my depleted energies. Although some were struck down and a few had even been eaten alive, they kept on crusading. Arrows rained down upon our enemies from above, scimitars gutted them from below. Blood and entrails flooded the battlefield until we were ankle-deep in a mucky swamp of steaming gore.

The battle lasted for an extended time; I could hardly breathe, but I kept on getting bursts of energy from slaughtering my enemies. It was as if I were in a virtual reality game. The action almost seemed to retreat into a type of slow motion. Visions of this unearthly crusade splashed my senses with such brutality, I edged closer to insanity with every second. Body parts flew past, foul excretions spurted life essences dissipated in every direction. I was in such a nightmarish onslaught that there was no way to tell whether we were winning or losing.

But then, there was a massive push from our rear flank as more of our soldiers came to life and joined the fray. They charged forward past those of us who were there from the start, replenishing our ranks. This new onslaught resulted in more casualties than this army of evil could bear. They couldn't help but notice their monstrous comrades being slain one by one as we battled. As the warring stretched on, we now saw fear in their otherworldly eyes. No one could guess what bizarre thoughts processed through their unearthly brains, but they obviously sensed they had lost this epic conflict once more.

Just as we thought we were victorious, a single frenzied abomination exploded with rage, refusing to retreat and suffer defeat. Whatever mind resided inside that warped, mishappen skull had snapped. Insanity radiated from its entire body. It was a slimy cephalopod with spiked arms that swung so fast they were barely visible to the naked eye, with screams so shrill that some soldiers fell to their knees, holding hands to their ears in agony. It went into some gonzo attack mode, with spastic motions so odd they confused my eyesight. Like a tornado of appendages flailing in a cosmic last stand, this creature tore apart our frontlines with the devastation of a thousand chainsaws running amok.

As my battle mates flew past me, wailing as their sliced-off limbs followed them through the air, I steeled myself and charged. On my first strike, my sword shattered in a hail of steel shards. My hand and forearm blazed with mind-numbing agony. But I couldn't stop now. Spotting a knight's lance sticking out from the muck, I crawled over and snatched it up. I pointed it forward and splashed ahead through the foul pool of blood and guts at full speed, jamming the pointed end up into its abdomen. It tensed up in shock, so I twisted it around to cause greater damage.

The Viking saw what I was attempting and joined in. He grabbed hold of the lance with me, and together we rammed it deeper and deeper into its gut. The beast cried out and stumbled back. The other monsters observed what was happening and stopped dead in their tracks. Other warriors noticed our advance and charged forward. More slashing of blades and flailing of lost limbs ensued.

The Viking and I took advantage of their momentary pause. We pushed at the crazed creature, forcing it to stumble back. The African princess raced up and slammed her spear into it. The Knight slashed and gouged it with his sword. It threw its head back, its face squeezing into a death mask, and it finally fell, and would breathe no more.

This signaled the end of this skirmish. The remaining beasts fled back to their haunted dimension on the other side of the hatch. But what would stop them from regrouping and attacking once more?

“We must follow them to the other side,” the Viking howled.

“That’s the only way to truly stop them,” the Knight concurred.

“We’ve had a good run these past centuries. Now follow me,” the African princess shouted.

This ebon heroine launched herself towards the portal, battling back the last remnants of this evil army across the threshold. The Viking and Knight joined in, leaping through the fractured metal gate and attacking them on their own ground. They kept fighting, preventing them from returning across to our Earth. On our side of the gate, we slaughtered whatever straggling beasts who had been left behind.

Somehow, the gateway made its own judgement, that our side had won. It began to glow, then the heat from it warmed the cave. The metal melded and reshaped, until it returned to its former stage as a barrier between the two dimensions. The trio of valiant warriors had been left on the other side. I watched through the gap in the gate till the very end. They kept the things at bay, away from the gate so it could heal itself.

A massive cry of victory echoed through the cave. The onslaught had ended.

It took quite a while for us victorious soldiers to gather up enough strength to talk amongst ourselves. I watched in awe as their wounds healed by themselves, as if some god-like forces were at work. But those who had perished remained dead. I counted seventeen in total, including the three who crossed over to assure our triumph. It was impossible to add up all the monsters we had killed, for many of them had been hacked into pieces and were impossible to count.

As I sat on a boulder regaining my breath, a few of the others approached.

"You fought bravely," the Native American Chief said.

"You are one of us now, forever," the Ninja said.

"No, thanks. I am really honored, but I'll be headed back home as soon as I catch my breath."

They all smiled at me.

"Sorry, buddy, but the hatchway to the Earth's surface is already closing by now," the American sergeant said.

Without even a goodbye, I jumped up and raced back up the tunnel as fast as I possibly could, desperate to get back to the life I had outside. As I reached the last turn of the tunnel, I realized I had arrived just in time to see the water from the lake start to return and the great door sliding shut. I almost attempted a dive through that last tiny opening but stopped myself at the last instant. I would have been sheared in half.

I returned to the others. They smirked a bit, but not too smugly.

I could tell they were impressed by my part in the war and respected my abilities. I was taken aback, for they were gathering up the corpses of the slain beasts and filleting them like slaughtered steer. Others were starting bonfires.

"You're not thinking what I think you're thinking, are you?" I asked.

"Some of these meats are very tasty. And give us sustenance for our long hibernation to come," the Chief said.

"What is this place?" I asked.

"This is The Portae, the portal to the other place," the Ninja said.

"Every three and a third years, a new champion is chosen by the Powers of Life and Death."

"Soon, they arrive here to replenish the Terra Sentinel forces."

"Every fifty years or so, the monsters break through the doorway and try to take over Earth. These wars have been repeating over and over since I arrived here five thousand years ago from Mesopotamia."

"They have been going on over fifty thousand years ago, when we first sailed to Australia," the Aborigine said.

"They have been happening since Atlantis was at its peak over one million years ago," the Atlantean said.

We celebrated. We had our feast. We buried our fallen comrades and erected monuments for each of them, including the three who perished on the other side. We took a moment to honor them.

Then, without another word, they all returned to their spots along the walls. I followed and took my place amongst this legion of valiant warriors. As the mysterious force began to transform us back into statues until we were needed once more, I noticed a sign carved into the wall at the entrance to the graveyard. These words were carved upon it.

"Only brutality by the good can prevent the advances of evil."

www.ingramcontent.com/pod-product-compliance
Lightning Source LLC
LaVergne TN
LVHW010629100826
845148LV00014B/3175
* 9 7 8 1 7 3 6 8 5 2 2 7 9 *